Failblog

Sheila Scobba Banning

A Carter Bros Mystery

For the "X" men

Chapter 1

"You're doing it wrong, loner! Here, let me show you."

Xander Carter grabbed the iPod from his younger brother and expertly thumbed the screen.

"Give it back!" Jackson shoved him but failed to retrieve the game. Waves of students swirled around them on their way to class.

"Here." Xander tossed the iPod dismissively onto the picnic table Jackson was leaning on and brushed straight blonde bangs off his forehead. "Just because I have standards. . . ." He grabbed his backpack and slung it over his shoulder, saluting as he walked away. "Late-ahs, bro."

"You're the loner." Jackson muttered as he resumed the game. Of course Xander actually had fixed the problem. Jackson was so good at sandbox and first person shooter games that he could usually beat even his older brother and his friends, but Xander had some kind of freaky affinity for the structure of the games, like he could see the code scrolling by. Or he was jacked into it. Or he was actually a machine. Sometimes it was useful, but it was also really really irritating. Always.

"Dude! C'mon. We're gonna be late."

Josh Rosen, star pitcher for the frosh baseball team and Jackson's best friend, grabbed his arm and hauled him away from the table toward their first class. Jackson walked backward while finishing his game, trusting Josh to guide him. They made it to History just as the bell rang and scrambled into their seats. Jackson smiled angelically at the teacher as the sound died away. He had the head of curls to go with the smile, but his were chestnut instead of golden.

Mrs. Mahoney shook her head. "Cutting it close again, Mr. Carter."

Jackson lifted his shoulders and pulled out his text book. "Sorry, Mrs. Mahoney." He flashed a halogen smile. "Won't happen again."

The teacher raised her eyebrows in disbelief. "I'm sure it won't, Jax." She began distributing papers around the classroom.

"Before we get to your current projects, let's go over last week's quiz."

Mrs. Mahoney returned to the front of the room when she had finished and opened the quiz folder on the smart board, then clicked on the corresponding icon for the paper she had just returned and the key filled the screen.

"There seemed to be some confusion on the first question, so I want to be sure you understand it before we move on. Lauren, would you . . ." the crackling of the classroom speaker cut her off and the room fell silent.

Everyone turned to face the box mounted in the corner of the room just as if it were an actual person speaking. Jackson exchanged looks with his friends, then watched the speaker again as if it might offer some visual clue to the unexpected interruption. It wasn't the usual time for announcements, and the room filled with suppressed energy, like the static electricity version of anticipation.

"All students and faculty please report to the gym immediately for a school-wide assembly." It was the voice of the principal, and she sounded shaken. "Again, please assemble in the gym now."

"Should we take our backpacks?" one of the girls in the back asked.

Mrs. Mahoney looked pale. "I don't know. I think it would be fine to leave them here." She took a deep breath. "Okay, class, let's go. Everybody up - and no running."

Jackson pulled out his phone and texted a question mark to his older brother. He didn't think Xander would reply, but figured it was worth a shot.

no clue

came back almost immediately. Jackson turned to Josh.

"If he doesn't know, nobody does."

"Or he might just be blowing you off," Josh said.

Jackson snorted. "True . . . but I don't think so. Not and miss the chance to show off."

They joined the streams of students pouring out of classrooms and moving toward the gym. Woodhaven High was a small private school built on the typical California model. One-story classrooms in an L-shape around an open field with the corridors covered only from above for protection during rainy season.

Lockers lined the corridors along the classroom walls, and the rest was open.

The pace of the students walking to assembly was a mix of rapid walking by those who were curious and wanted to find out what was going on and leisurely strolling by the ones who wanted to delay the return to class as long as possible. A few people stopped at their lockers or ducked into the restroom, a few more paused at the drinking fountain, but eventually they filled the wooden bleachers in the gym. Jackson and Josh spotted three of their friends and jostled onto the bleacher beside them.

Mrs. Johnson stood in the middle of the basketball court with a cordless microphone. She was a tiny woman with a helmet of white-blonde hair who always wore suits and platform heels. Today's suit was a beige tweed and the blouse she'd paired with it had a loosely-tied bow draping down between the lapels of her jacket. the silk loops bobbled as she made twitchy gestures. The school counselor towered over the Principal even in flats. Her serious face was completely visible even though she stood several feet behind along with an unknown fat woman in a bright pink dress. The muted conversations and squeaking bleachers began to get louder until Coach Ron walked in, closed the behind him, and nodded to the principal.

"May I have your attention, please. I am sorry to tell you that there has been a tragedy this morning. One of your former classmates . . ." her voice broke, but she swallowed hard and continued. "TJ Martin was killed last night at a CalTrain crossing. We don't have all the details, but the train couldn't stop in time, and they believe he died instantly."

The crowd was completely still now, and the only sound was sniffling and the occasional stifled sob.

Mrs. Johnson took a deep breath to continue. "Although TJ left Woodhaven High last week, we still think of him as part of the Woodhaven family." She gestured to the two women behind her. "Ms. Teeter and Dr. Laughton will be available all this week for anyone who needs to talk. Dr. Laughton is a grief specialist," she added by way of introduction. "You may return to your classes now."

"It's all your fault!" A girl at the far end of the gym stood up and pointed an accusing finger.

Gasps filled the gym.

"If you hadn't expelled him and ruined his life, TJ would be alive right now!" The girl was hysterical, her voice more shriek than shout. Everyone craned to get a better look. Mrs. Johnson's face was frozen somewhere between anger and guilt.

The grief counselor took the microphone from the principal.

"Blame is a perfectly normal response to a tragic loss." She smiled and held out her hand. "Why don't you come with me to the library conference room? Ms. Teeter will take any questions you have now and will be in her office all day, as well. Please do come talk with us."

The soothing tone diffused the situation. The girl collapsed onto the bleachers, sobbing into her hands as her friends crowded around comforting her. Everyone else around them practically ran for the door to escape the drama. Xander was one of them.

Jackson and his gang caught up to Xander and his friends.

"Who was that?" Jackson asked.

"Emily," Xander said.

"Yeah, she was all upset last week after TJ got kicked out," Xander's best friend Ben added. "Girl drama."

Xander frowned in thought. "She did say he was set up when it happened, remember? Tried to convince the administration that it must have been a practical joke and then spent most of lunch in the girl's restroom when they blew her off."

"How do you know that?" Josh asked.

Xander offered a smug smile and raised his eyebrows.

Jackson shook his head. "Don't even ask. But what practical joke? I heard he was drinking on campus."

"I heard he got caught trying to spike the punch at the spirit rally," Jackson's friend Ethan said.

"I heard he had a full bar in his locker," Xander's friend Reza added.

Xander cut them off. "The water bottle in his locker was filled with vodka. He admitted it was his bottle, but denied the alcohol was his." He shrugged. "Zero tolerance."

"Harsh." Jackson shook his head. "I mean, the guy was an honor student, right? On the Student Council?"

"ZERO tolerance, doof. Not zero except for good kids. Do you even know the number zero?"

"Zero is a concept, not a number." Jackson smirked at Xander in the way that usually got him punched in the arm but was totally worth it.

"Guys, guys," Matthew said, "can we move on to class before we all get detention?"

"They won't give us detention for coming back too slowly. Not right now, anyway. We've probably got a full school day of slack, maybe two," Jackson said.

"I feel really bad for his parents," Jackson's friend Nicholas said as the Juniors and Freshmen parted ways. "His dad brought him lunch that day he was kicked out. He must be really broken up."

Xander stopped abruptly and turned around. His entourage stopped with him.

"What did you say?"

Nicholas was small and shy. He flinched in response to Xander's inquisition.

"TJ's dad brought him lunch. Last week. I was getting a book out of my locker during Lit and he asked me if he was in the right place."

Jackson's friends and Xander's all looked at him. "Why do you care?" Jackson asked.

Xander looked him in the eye.

"TJ didn't have a dad."

Chapter 2

"What? But he talked to me." Nicholas looked confused, which was not unusual.

"He brought lunch."

"Fail!" Jackson said. "He means that guy might have brought lunch, but he couldn't have been TJ's dad."

"But . . . why would he lie to me?"

"That's exactly what I was thinking," Xander said.

"What is going on here, boys? Todo bien?"

Senora Sanchez walked up to the group with a concerned expression.

"Hola, Senora," Xander said, brushing his sun-streaked hair off his face. "We were just going."

"Classes are resuming, Alejandro, you need to move along."

"We stopped to see when the counselor is available," Jackson said. He lowered his eyes. "Lo siento, Senora"

Her face crumpled. "No, no, mijo, no need to be sorry. You boys are fine."

Josh and Nicholas low-fived behind Jackson's back when Senora wasn't looking. Xander threw him a look half irritation half admiration, which was pretty much how he felt about Jackson all the time. He could not believe the stuff that kid got away with. He was like a Jedi Master of dealing with adults.

"Gracias, Senora. We'll hurry."

Xander was already in the car waiting by the time Jackson stopped at his locker to exchange books for the next day's classes.

"Jax! " He yelled, leaning out the driver's window. "Hurry up!"

Jackson loped over to the black and tan 1977 Mustang Ghia, tossed his backpack into the narrow back seat, and dropped into the front passenger seat with a thud.

"Hey!" Xander said indignantly. "Did you put all your savings into this car? Did you work on it for six months?"

Jackson didn't even look over. "Bill me."

Xander started to launch into an argument, but started the car, instead, and the engine growled into a deep V8 rumble that had been tweaked into something deeper than a purr. He was backing out of the parking space into the exit line before Jackson had finished fastening his seat belt.

"Dude! What the heck?"

"We need to make a little Starbucks detour on the way home I want to talk to Emily and this is her day at Children's Hospital. We've only got until 3:45."

Jackson pressed his earbuds into place and started thumbing the screen furiously.

"I want to see the intersection where TJ was killed, too."

"What?" He pulled out an earbud as Xander repeated his statement. "Oh, man! Can't you drop me at home first?"

"I could," Xander said, "but since it's in the opposite direction, I'm not going to. Feel free to walk home from Starbuck's."

"What, like five miles? Thank you sooooo much. I think I'll pass on that generous offer, bro." Jackson screwed the earbud back into place and resumed playing.

A few minutes later they pulled into a parking spot across from Starbuck's and Xander got out of the car.

"You coming?" he asked.

Jackson didn't look up from his game. "Nah."

Xander closed his door and started toward the coffee shop.

"Wait!" Jackson said, shoving his iPod into his pocket and locking his door.

Xander rolled his eyes. "Do you ever NOT change your mind?"

"Yeah. I'm always certain you're a jerk."

Xander walked into Starbuck's ahead of Jackson and scanned the tables for Emily. The place was full of the usual after school crowd, elementary school kids with their moms, clusters of moms child-free while their kids no doubt had some sport practice or club, and a handful of retired people who had the misfortune of lingering past dismissal time.

"I don't see her."

The restroom door opened and Emily lifted her hand. Her eyes were red and she wasn't wearing any make-up. She didn't usually wear much, anyway, but she had clearly given up on mascara for the day.

"Can I get you something?" Xander asked.

Emily shook her head, then hesitated and looked at the menu board. "Maybe just an iced tea. She looked around. "I'll get a seat outside."

"I'll have a vanilla bean smoothie," Jackson said.

Xander handed him a plastic gift card. "Yeah, me too. You get them and bring them out, okay?"

Jackson started to refuse, then realized he was getting his drink paid for. "Sure."

Emily had chosen the furthest table from the door, around the corner next to a vacant storefront. She paused mid-sentence when Jackson walked up with the drinks, thanked him, and continued.

"Bitter and angry aren't the same thing as suicidal. Or I didn't think they were." She blinked back tears as she sipped from her drink and then rattled the ice in the plastic cup. "He tried to tell

Mrs. Johnson that he hadn't seen that water bottle in a couple weeks, but she wouldn't even listen."

"Zero tolerance," Jackson said.

"Yeah. Except it should be whoever put it there who was kicked out, not TJ. They didn't even try to find out. Said his locker was locked like that was evidence."

Xander frowned. "Was his mom really mad?"

"Well, sure, but not like throw him out of the house mad. I mean, it was a big deal to go from golden boy to expelled, but it's not like he was in any other trouble. He told me Saturday . . ." this time she broke down, crying in earnest and digging through her purse for a tissue.

Jackson shifted uncomfortably in his seat and looked out to the parking lot, but Xander just waited patiently. When she had dried her face and gotten her breathing under control, he said, "You talked to TJ Saturday?"

Emily nodded and hiccuped. "On the phone. He said he found some statement in the Honor Code about a fair hearing." She looked down, stifling another hiccup. "It didn't sound like he had given up. He sounded . . . hopeful. But maybe the school turned him down?"

She took a ragged breath and stood up, grabbing her bag.

"I have to go. Thanks for the drink, Xander. See you, Jax."

Xander continued to stare off into the space Emily had occupied until Jackson ran a hand in front of his face.

"Earth to Xander."

Instead of the expected smartass response or physical retribution, Xander turned to Jackson and asked, "How many people do you know who lock their lockers?"

Woodhaven had a reputation for being a safe place. A laptop left out on a picnic table at lunch was still there after school. Anything valuable left out at the end of the day was taken to the office by the maintenance staff. Most kids blocked the latches on their lockers to save time, because who was going to take anything?

Jackson thought about Xander's question. "Maybe five. All girls." He shrugged. "And I don't even want to know what that's about."

"Yeah, that sounds about right." He shot his empty cup into the trash can like a free throw. "Let's go."

The V8 thrummed as Xander shifted gears and turned off the expressway onto the first street that would take them cross town to the CalTrain tracks. There were many intersections from Mountain View to Atherton with train crossings, but the one where TJ was found had seen half a dozen deaths. Though there hadn't been any in the last couple years, the spot was infamous for a teenage suicide cluster of four high school students in as many months.

Xander drove across the tracks and through the intersection, then made a U-turn and waited at the light to cross back the other way. He turned onto a frontage road just on the other side of the tracks and parked. It wouldn't make any sense to run all the way across the road to step in front of a train. He had to have been on this side.

"Why here?" Xander said to himself.

Jackson looked up from his game. "You mean, what kind of idiot uses a train to commit suicide?"

"Blog! There's that, too." Xander got out of the car and Jackson followed. "But if you're going to do it, why go so far out of your way? This isn't the closest train crossing to his house."

The boys walked around the fence to stand beside the tracks, drawing funny looks from the passengers in the passing cars. Jackson smiled and waved.

"Try not to look suicidal," he said, shoving Xander. "you're making the commuters nervous." Jackson watched as Xander scuffed the rubble around the warning arm with his toe and looked up and down tracks. "What are you looking for?"

"I don't know . . . let's go to the other side where the flowers are."

They waited for the light to change again and hold the traffic, then dashed across the street between the stopped cars. Bouquets of flowers and individual stems had been woven into the wire mesh of the fence next to the road. As the boys made it to that side, the warning lights began clanging and the guardrail dropped. Xander covered his ears and leaned back against the fence as the train blew past. Jackson shielded his eyes with one hand to keep out the grit and trash stirred up in the wake of the train. Flower petals flew by and notes fluttered against the fence.

"Hey! You kids! What are you doing?"

A large man in a dark blue zippered jacket and matching cap yelled at them from across the road. The jacket had a patch that looked like CalTrain, but it was hard to tell from that distance.

Xander walked further up the tracks and dropped to one knee. "Let's go!" Jackson said. He turned to face the man who was watching for an opening in the traffic and waved one arm in the air.

"Sorry, sir, we were just leaving." He looked and sounded contrite. "Get up, Xander!" his practically spit out of the side of his mouth before smiling broadly and walking toward the man.

"This isn't a tourist attraction, it's a dangerous place. There will not be any copycats on my watch." His voice got louder as he got closer, starting as a surly grumble and ending with a shout.

"We just wanted to leave something - " Jackson's voice caught " something for TJ . . ." he swallowed and looked at the ground, shaking his head slowly. He heard Xander walking up behind him and felt a surge of relief.

"I'm sorry for your loss, boys," the security guard, if that's what he was, lowered his volume but remained firm, "but you'll have to go now."

"Okay," Xander said. "Sorry for the trouble."

The boys didn't speak while the guard walked them back to their car. As soon as they pulled away from the intersection, Xander reached over and dropped something in Jackson's lap.

"What the heck?"

Jackson picked up the small plastic oval and examined it. It was pretty scraped up, but there was no mistaking what it was. Xander had a Nike+ sensor just like it on his shoelaces.

"Is that what you were doing instead of running? Fixing your stupid shoe?"

"No. My sensor is still on. I think this one belonged to TJ."

"So?"

Xander pressed his lips together in a grim smile. "So I'm going to hack into his sync account and see what he was up to before he died."

Chapter 3

"Hey, Mom, we're home!" Jackson yelled as they walked through the atrium and opened the glass door to the living room.

Xander turned to him. "She's working, loser. How often does she hear you and answer you?"

Jackson scrunched his face in thought. "I think I remember one time. No, wait! Two!"

Xander shook his head in disgust. "So why do you bother?"

"Do you remember the time she just about had a heart attack and accused us of sneaking up on her?"

"Yeah . . . ." Xander wondered where he was going.

Jackson poked a finger into Xander's chest. "Plausible deniability." He grinned.

Xander rolled his eyes and started toward his room. "Weirdo. You come up with some genuinely creepy stuff."

"I'll take that as a compliment!" Jackson yelled after his brother. He went to the kitchen to grab a banana and a Vitamin Water before going to do his homework. He heard the garage door slam and walked into the dining room.

"Hey, Mom."

"Hi, Baby! How was your day?"

Mona Carter reached up to hug her son. She smelled like lavender, jasmine and hot glue. Her gray-streaked auburn hair was held loosely on top of her head with a clip. The faded blue shirt she was wearing would have matched her eyes if it hadn't been covered with slashes of paint, ink splatters, and what looked like resistors trapped in dried glue like beetles in amber. She had a long strand of electroluminescent wire looped around her wrist.

"Good," Jackson said. "And odd," he added.

"Odd how?" Mona searched his face. "What happened?"

"Remember the guy who was expelled last week?"

Mona scrunched her face in thought. "Maybe . . ."

"He was killed by a train last night. Or early this morning." Jackson shrugged. "I don't remember what they said."

"Oh my god!" Mona squeezed his arm. "Are you okay? Was it . . . suicide?"

Jackson opened the vitamin water and drank half of it. "The school thinks so. They brought in a counselor."

"The school thinks so?" She watched him peel the banana. "What do you think?"

"I think I've got homework." Jackson grinned, hefted his backpack onto his shoulder and backed out of the room wiggling his fingers.

Mona shook her head then followed in his wake through the living room and down the hall. She stopped at Xander's room and knocked on the open door.

He looked over his shoulder without lifting his fingers from his laptop keyboard.

"Hey, Mom." He took in the green tube around her wrist and the glue bits on her shirt. "What are you working on?"

Mona walked into the room. "I'm thinking about a series of canvases with motion sensors incorporated so walking past activates one light sequence and standing still causes it to revert to the original."

"Cool."

"I just haven't decided on the power source and whether I want the piece to have a life cycle or be rechargeable and permanent."

"I vote permanent plug-in," Xander said. "Who wants a dead painting hanging on their wall."

"Speaking of dead . . . ." Mona walked around to stand beside the desk facing Xander.

Xander clicked on a new window and turned toward her. "No. You did not just say that!"

"Sorry, that was a pretty tacky segue." Mona touched his hair and he leaned away. "I just wanted to see how you're doing. Jackson told me about the assembly today."

"I figured." Xander said. "I'm okay, I guess."

"You guess?"

He turned back to his computer and squinted at the screen without typing. "The whole TJ thing just doesn't add up."

Mona put her hand on his shoulder. "Suicide never adds up to the people left behind. You can't know what he was thinking or feeling."

"Thinking and feeling . . .thinking and feeling!" Xander straightened in his chair. "Thanks, Mom. Gotta get back to my homework."

"Okay, sweetie."

Mona walked back to the kitchen. She knew that look. Xander with a puzzle was like a terrier with a rat. He just couldn't leave it alone, and everyone around him got sucked into the obsession along with him. Or at least had to suffer through his relentless quest. She hoped he would find out something about the suicide that would satisfy him enough to move on to something else. And she hoped it would happen without him pestering the poor boy's mother. She wouldn't plant the idea by saying so though.

Make meatloaf or order pizza? She checked the clock. She had time for meatloaf. Mona turned on the water then spotted the el-wire wrapped around her arm. "Whoops!" She took it out to her garage studio, washed her hands and started dinner.

"Pass the ketchup, Jax."

"Excuse me?" Mona said.

"Please." Xander added.

"Please what?" Jackson grinned.

"Please hand me the ketchup before I pound your face in."

"Ahem." Mona fake cleared her throat and gave them a look. "Don't threaten him," she said to Xander then turned to Jackson. "He said please."

Jackson passed the ketchup, holding onto it long enough to create a brief tug of war.

Mona sighed.

"Is there going to be a memorial for your friend?"

"Prob'ly." Xander answered while wolfing down his second piece of meatloaf. "Are there more mashed potatoes?"

"No," Mona said. "but you can have the rest of mine."

"Ewww! Mom cooties!" Xander made a face.

"Lovely," Mona said.

"Don't be so mean!" Jackson said.

"JK." Xander held up his hands as if in surrender then scraped the small mound of potatoes off her plate. "Thanks, Mom." He ate with a focus. "When is Dad coming home?" he asked without looking up.

"A couple more days," Mona answered. "He should be calling in a little while though. You guys done with homework?"

"Just drum practice left," Jackson said.

Mona shook her head as she watched the boys eat. Even though it had been a good five years since the puberty train left the station, the endless shoveling of coal into the engines never seemed to end. She thought there must be a piece in that, a painting with parallel lines and blinking lights and an actual heat source . . . then that image was erased and replaced with the image of one of her boys on the train tracks - and the lights winking out one by one. She took a deep, uneven breath.

"Mom?" Jackson looked worried. "Are you okay?"

Mona nodded and smiled. "I was just thinking about a work in progress."

He studied her face for a moment, knowing she wasn't telling him everything, then asked, "Is there any dessert?"

Much later that night after their mom was in bed, Jackson crept out into the hallway. He could see the glow of Xander's iPad in the dark. Sometimes the advantages and disadvantages of living in a house with glass walls were exactly the same. He eased the door open and leaned in.

"Well?

"Listen to this," Xander said without looking up, "TJ wasn't an over-sharer, but he did check-in from the Coffee House at Stanford last night at nine-thirty. I'm looking at his private messages now to see if any were sent or received around then."

"His messages? How did you get in?"

Xander answered without looking up. "All his childhood pets, favorite sports, teams, bands, songs, and foods are on his Timeline. I wrote an algorithm to test passwords using standard symbol substitutions like the 'at' symbol for 'a' and the number one or an exclamation point for 'l' and 'i' and let it run until I got in."

Jackson sat on the edge of the bed watching Xander frown at the screen wearing his yellow-tinted gamer glasses. "Just promise me you'll always use your powers for good."

Xander smirked for a second without breaking concentration. "No messages, but if he talked to anyone, he was probably texting." He paused and looked intently through Jackson for a moment. "I wonder if we could get his phone . . . ." then he dropped his eyes back to his work, clicking back and forth between two windows and typing furiously. "Here's the weird thing, though . . ." He flipped the laptop around so Jackson could see the screen.

"What am I looking at?" Jackson asked, "a math problem? It looks like a bar graph."

"According to his Nike plus sync account, he didn't take any steps at all after about 10:10." Xander turned the computer back and frowned thoughtfully at the screen, his face bathed in a bluish glow.

"Do we know what time he was . . . hit?"

"It was the 10:36 Southbound," Xander said with a grim expression.

"The news blurb didn't say anything about a bike."

Xander looked at him and nodded. "Somebody else drove him there.

Chapter 4

"What do you mean TJ didn't kill himself?" Xander's friend Reza asked between giant bites of his turkey sub. He pointed at Xander's sandwich. "Is that turkey bacon?"

"Pork. None for you." Xander put down his BLT and took a big gulp of Vitamin Water. He was holding court at the end of a picnic table filled with Juniors eating lunch and doing homework, some standing, some sitting, some milling around. He picked up a grape from his plate and threw it high in the air. Reza caught it in his mouth. "I mean I think the whole thing smells like your gym bag."

"Ew! Nasty!" One of the girls standing behind the table tossed a pencil at Xander. He blocked it with his hands, then picked up his sandwich.

"Sorry, Katrina. But seriously," he turned back to the table, "this whole thing with TJ is messed up. Starting with his expulsion. That sports bottle full of vodka was obviously planted."

"Obviously?" Ben asked.

"Loner! Yeah, obviously," Xander said. " Vodka? TJ? Really?"

Xander surveyed the faces of his friends. Woodhaven might be in the middle of the Bay Area, but it had the feel of a small town. Everybody knew everybody else, at least a little, and personal quirks were accepted without much more than harmless ribbing. When everyone is weird somehow, no one is an outsider. Reza looked like a basketball player, but his real love was jazz guitar. Ben was a faculty brat with so much arcane knowledge of WWII that even the faculty consulted him, and Matthew baked all the treats for end of season parties. But friends or not, Xander could tell they weren't buying his theory.

"And I don't believe he jumped in front of that train either."

Matthew stood up to dump his plate in the trash. "So, what, then? He was pushed?

"Maybe."

"If you think that, why don't you go to the police?"

"Failblog!" Xander scoffed openly at his friend. "You guys barely believe me; can you imagine what the police would say?" He took another bite and chewed a couple times, drumming his fingertips on the table like an invisible keyboard. "I have to get more evidence."

Ben looked up from his furious note copying. "Evidence? What?"

Xander balled up his napkin and bounced it off Ben's forehead. "Yeah. Facts. Concrete. Provable. Non-dismissible."

The first bell rang, and everyone scrambled to dispose of their trash and collect their belongings. Matthew stopped beside Xander before they parted for class.

"I need to tell you something." He looked over Xander's shoulder then over his own, up and down the open corridors from the picnic tables to the office and back down toward the lockers and junior high classrooms. "I saw TJ that night before he went out. He asked me to bring a hard copy of the Student Handbook because he lost online access when he was expelled."

36

Xander adjusted his backpack and turned toward Matthew. His friend was flushed, his eyes darting.

"You are totally right. There's no way he killed himself!"

Weirdly, his voice dropped in volume as it became more intense, so he was almost hissing more than talking.

"But he didn't care about the Honor Code anymore when I got there. He was all excited about some meeting he had that night, some big plan to take care of his mom for the rest of her life." Matthew looked at his shoes and shook his head, then jerked his head up as the second bell rang. "He said being expelled was the best thing that ever happened to him."

Xander punched Matthew's arm. "That was worth getting a tardy for, man. Thanks."

"Xander? Mr. Carter?"

Xander was startled back to the classroom by the voice of his teacher. "Um . . . forty-two?" He offered a toothy exaggerated grin to simultaneously acknowledge that he'd been caught not paying attention and beg for mercy.

Ms. Wilder shook her head and stifled a smile. "While I appreciate your attempt to reach back into the dim recesses of literature to come up with an answer I might appreciate, this is psychology, not philosophy."

"Could you repeat the question." There were snickers from Xander's friends. "Please?"

"How would you explain Maslow's hierarchy?"

"Maslow?" Xander's eyebrows shot up in surprised relief. Something he actually knew. Cheated death again. "Well . . . he's saying that if you haven't met your basic needs, like if you're hungry or out of work or alone in the world, you can't really achieve your highest intellectual or emotional capacity."

"And why is that, Justin?" The teacher turned to another student.

"Uh . . . if you're worried about eating or surviving, you can't think about more complicated stuff?"

"I don't think that's true, though!" Xander blurted out.

The teacher cleared her throat. Xander raised his hand and waited to be acknowledged.

"Sorry, Ms. Wilder. I think some of the self-actualization qualities he lists for becoming the best person you can be have to be there all along, like morality and problem solving and even creativity. How do you feed yourself or get a job if you don't have those things to begin with?" Xander paused. "But what I really wonder is how suicide fits with his pyramid."

The teacher sighed, but nodded as if the question were expected.

"Suicide is difficult for most psychologists to fully explain, because individual motivations differ, but they usually look for mental illness or severe depression. In Maslow's case, a loss anywhere on the pyramid, if severe enough, could cause the whole structure to crumble."

Xander nodded and looked at the graphic in his textbook. There wasn't a single brick out of TJ's pyramid that he could see. The administration probably thought he was depressed about his expulsion, but TJ had been mounting a defense. No doubt some of them thought he was secretly being bullied for being gay or something equally topical, but neither was true, as far as Xander knew. And Matthew said TJ was excited about something.

Something that happened after he got expelled . . . Xander needed to get his phone. And a new app.

"Jax! Jackson!" Xander called over the crowd noise in the corridor during the break between classes. Jackson paused and Xander caught up to him. "Tell your friend Nicholas I need to see him after school."

"Which Nicholas?"

"The one who saw the guy looking for TJ's locker."

"He's got baseball every day," Jackson said. "What do you want him for?"

"I need a better description. Okay, if he can't do after school . . ." Xander ran through his own schedule mentally, "tell him to meet me in the library tomorrow at lunch time." He turned to go, then turned back. "You'd better bring him. Just to make sure he gets there."

Jackson smiled. Nicholas was a nice guy, but in a universe of his own, which had led to a well-deserved reputation for unreliability. "Why should I?"

Xander sighed. "If you get him there, you can stay and watch. Deal?"

Jackson scrunched his face as if doing complex calculations.

"Deal?" Xander demanded.

"Yeah. That might be amusing."

As Xander walked away he coughed "Loner!" into his hand.

"Fail! Do you even know what that means?" Jackson shook his head and went to class.

"Nicholas says he'll meet you, but he can't do it until Thursday," Jackson told Xander during the drive home, "and he said he doesn't remember anything, anyway."

Xander snorted. "That doesn't surprise me. But trust me, he remembers more than he thinks he does. He just needs a little computer assistance."

Xander pulled into the driveway and revved the engine a couple times before turning off the car.

"You know Dan and Lisa hate that, right?" Jackson said as they collected their backpacks and Xander locked the doors.

"I know. It's payback for calling the police about our music being too loud last summer. Who does that? They've known us for our entire lives and they can't just ask us to turn it down?"

Jackson shook his head as they walked through the atrium. "What are you, the elephant of resentment?"

"Ha. Ha. That's almost funny," Xander said.

They heard music coming from the garage as they walked in. It stopped when Jackson closed the sliding glass door and their mom came in to greet them. She handed an early wasabi green iPod to Xander.

"You were listening to my iPod?"

Mona shrugged. "I like to keep up on your musical taste. Since when does Nietzsche write pop music?"

The boys both looked at the screen to see what she had been listening to. Jackson burst into a loud falsetto, singing "What doesn't kill me makes me stronger . . ." as he danced around with his arms in the air.

Xander blushed. "Jennifer loaded that. Don't go buying me any albums."

"Ah." Mona smiled. "Well, I liked it anyway. So how was your day?" She looked from one boy to the other. "Anything new?"

Xander shot Jackson a glance, but he didn't catch the meaning. "Fine. Speaking of new . . . will you buy me a pattern recognition app?"

"Is it for school?"

"It's for a project."

"And I assume you don't want to buy it with your own money because you just bought another motion sensor camera, wireless mouse or attachments for your Google glasses?"

Xander looked sheepish. "Pretty much."

"Well . . ."

"We're designing a crossover project between math and psychology using facial features and pattern recognition," Jackson said.

"Oh! Like a variation on facial recognition?" Mona asked. "Are you both working on it?"

They answered simultaneously.

"Yes."

"No."

Xander looked at Jackson and changed his answer. "Yes. We're not doing everything together, but we're both using it."

"Okay, then. Use my PayPal account."

"I'll bring you the laptop to do your password as soon as I've got the order done," Xander said.

As the boys walked down the hall toward their bedrooms, Jackson said in a low voice, "Fail! Don't you know mom's password?"

"Of course I do." Xander smiled. "But if I ever used it without permission, that would be the LAST time I got to use it. I'm saving that nuclear option for an emergency."

Chapter 5

"There's something wrong with his nose."

Nicholas squinted at the face on Xander's iPad and tilted his head to the side. His short dark hair stood up on the right side where he hadn't been able to brush the aftershocks of sleep out of it.

Jackson muttered, "Fail!" under his breath and sighed. Nicholas had gone from certain he couldn't help them to excited about seeing the face develop on the screen to obsessing about details he had initially said he couldn't remember. The app was pretty sick, but his enthusiasm had waned the further off course Nicholas went. Xander wasn't losing patience, though, he just kept adjusting the image and asking questions.

"Okay," Xander said. "Close your eyes and tell us again what happened that day."

Nicholas closed his eyes. "I was going back to class from my locker, and a man came up the main path from the parking lot."

"How was he dressed?" Xander asked. "Jeans? Khakis? Suit? Uniform?"

Nicholas squeezed his eyes and furrowed his brow. "Collared shirt and dark pants."

"Collared shirt business or engineer?" Jackson asked.

Nicholas opened his eyes. "What?"

"Starched-collar money guy or frayed button-down software guy?"

Xander shot Jackson a look to cut him off and leaned in toward Nicholas. "Go on."

Nicholas closed his eyes again. "He looked surprised to see me. He held up the bag in his hand and said he brought TJ's lunch."

"Did he actually say he was TJ's dad?"

Nicholas nodded.

"Okay," Xander said, "now open your eyes and look at the screen again. Don't look at the details, just anything that stands out as wrong."

"It's not the nose. The eyes should be closer together and the eyebrows thicker. And make the mouth smile. He smiled the whole time. Like a movie star."

"Movie star?" Xander asked.

"You mean really white teeth or you mean like he probably smiled all the time but didn't mean it?" Jackson added.

"That second one," Nicholas said.

Xander nodded. "Thanks," he said, closing the iPad and dismissing them both. "I'll let you know if I need anything else."

He stood up and strode out of the library. The two freshmen trailed in his wake.

"That was kind of fun," Nicholas said, "but I still don't get what he was doing it for."

Jackson put his hand on his friend's shoulder. "Dude? With my brother, that is always the question."

The very second the dismissal bell rang, Xander's phone pinged with a text message.

bk lockers... now

It was from Jackson. Xander was automatically irritated, but the excitement of the location overrode his standard response to his brother. He wanted to meet at the block where TJ's locker was.

"Dude? Black Ops?" Ben came up behind Xander and nudged him as he checked on after school online game plans.

"Loner!" Xander responded automatically. "Yeah. Prob'ly later. Come with me for a sec."

Ben shrugged under the weight of his backpack and followed without asking questions. Whatever Xander was up to was always interesting, and it wasn't like there was anything else going on right then.

The two juniors rounded the corner from the main corridor, passed the picnic tables, and turned down the path to the back lockers. Jackson and his friends were there along with a couple kids packing up for the day.

Xander walked up to his brother and made a dipping gesture with his right hand that Jackson faded back to evade. "What?" Xander asked with extra contempt to hide his interest.

"Nicholas remembered something."

Nicholas shrank back, then stood up straight. He only came up to Xander's chest. "Money. Definitely money!"

Xander looked from Jackson to Ben and back again. "Money?" he asked Nicholas with a tonal uplift and exasperated inflection that demanded more information.

Nicholas smiled broadly. "Like Jax said before." When no one responded he added. "The shirt. Starched. And the cuffs had a monogram."

"What?" Xander practically shrieked, then dialed back when Nicholas flinched. "Sorry. What do you mean there was a monogram?"

Jackson wore a smug smirk. "When he thought about what I'd asked about the shirt at lunch, it came back to him."

Nicholas nodded. "The shirt was just white, but when he pointed to the lockers, I noticed the dark blue letters." He shook his head before Xander could ask. "I couldn't read them, though. But the shirt was . . ." he looked at Jackson, " . . . crisp? Like what Josh's dad wears when he's not coaching."

Josh raised his eyebrows. "Hey, leave my dad out of this."

"Whaleblog!" Jackson said. "He didn't say it *was* your dad!"

"What's your dad do?" Xander asked Josh. "Venture? Finance?"

"Yeah. Financial something."

Xander raised his eyebrows at his brother, and they said in unison, "Sand Hill Road."

memorial tomorrow reception after at TJ home   Xander typed. It was after midnight and the only light in the room came from his computer screen.

anything? Jackson typed back.

skype

Xander and Jackson put on their headsets and set up the skype connection despite the fact that they were separated by a single wall and about twenty feet. Their dad had come home in time to have a quick dinner with them before jet lag caught up with him. Still, he somehow heard the opening and closing of any door in the house, no matter how tired he was, so Jackson and Xander rarely did late night face time when he was home.

"Has the face recognition software come up with anything?" Jackson asked.

Xander adjusted his mic. "I'm not expecting anything until at least tomorrow. The program's running, though. I have to keep setting up new files. If Woodhaven had photos in the directory, it would make things easier."

"You really think it was a parent?"

"Maybe not, but the guy had definitely been on campus before."

"How many have you done?"

"All the school photo sharing sites have run, the gala photos, awards ceremonies and sports candids. I had one hit, but it turned out to be somebody's mom."

"Fail!" Jackson snorted. "That's just sad. . . . so what about the memorial?"

"We're going. I offered to drive Emily and Matthew, since they were friends."

"Nice."

"I want to get a shot at his phone, maybe grab the sim card. If that's not an option, I'll go for his laptop."

"And why do I have to go to this?" Jackson asked.

"In case I need you to talk to his mom."

The next day dragged until the final bell. The Carter brothers converged on the old Mustang from opposite ends of campus. Matthew walked with Xander, slipping a pre-tied necktie over his head and adjusting it under the collar of his shirt as they walked. Emily caught up to them just as they reached the car, her black cotton dress emphasized her pale face. Xander unlocked the trunk so they could stash their backpacks.

"Shotgun!" Jackson said.

"Really?" Xander asked in a voice dripping with sarcasm as he shot a withering look. "Emily is sitting in front."

Jackson blushed. "Right. Sorry."

They arranged themselves in the car and Xander pulled the two slightly crumpled silk ties off of the review mirror and tossed one into the back seat, then looped the other over his own neck. The group traveled in silence to the Stanford campus where TJ's mom worked in student services. The memorial was being held at Dinkelspiel Auditorium near the student union, and Xander circled the Tresidder lot for a metered space before giving up and letting everyone else out near Dink so he could troll for parking out on the street. He considered parking in one of the staff spots, but the little parking patrol cart pulled in just as he approached it, so he resisted temptation.

By the time he made it inside, the auditorium was packed. There were still students and a few Woodhaven faculty trailing in from their similar adventures in parking, but the seats were filled with Mrs. Martin's friends and colleagues who had walked from various campus locations. Xander squeezed in between Matthew and Emily standing at the back. There was a brief video with photos of TJ's life followed by a string trio playing a piece he had written for the talent show. There was much stifled sniffling and some open sobbing throughout the group of mourners, but Xander was dry-eyed, frowning hard at the video screen with a recent photo of TJ frozen in an endless smile.

When everyone who wanted to speak about TJ was finished, Mrs. Martin thanked them for coming and invited them all back to the house. Xander lifted his chin at Jackson over Emily's head.

"Let's go."

Jackson knew the look. "Where are we going?"

"The CoHo is right across the plaza from here," Xander said.

"So?" Matthew asked.

Xander and Jackson both looked at Emily then at each other.

"Um . . .latte," Jackson said, "for the road."

"But you guys can wait at the picnic tables, if you don't want anything," Xander added. "And I can bring the car around, if you want." He ran one hand through his hair.

Emily's eyes were red-rimmed and seemed to be focused somewhere else. When friends and family were making testimonials to TJ, she had taken a step toward the aisle, then stepped back and looked at the floor shaking her head, unable to bring herself to speak. She paused by the tables. "No," she said to Xander, "we can walk together. Sitting for a minute would be nice."

Emily swayed a little as she started to sit, and Jackson took her arm to guide her down. Matthew sat and put his arm around her, nodding to Xander.

The brothers walked into the coffee house and got in line. There were college students scattered around the room at tables and the narrow bar around the service area, but their fellow mourners hadn't yet started clogging the room. When they reached the register, Jackson ordered a strawberry smoothie and Xander asked for a latte.

"Since when do you drink lattes?" Jackson asked.

"Since you said we were getting one, loser."

The server gave them the total and Xander gave Jackson a look. Jackson rolled his eyes, shook his head, and pulled out his wallet. While he was paying, Xander pulled out his phone.

"We were just at the memorial," he said as the lanky guy with dreads made change. "Did you know TJ?" He showed him a photo.

"Oh, yeah, that kid! He comes in pretty often." The barrista blanched. "I mean . . . . he used to. We talked about classes, dorms, stuff like that." He shook his head. "He said he was applying. His mom works here." He turned away to get the drinks.

"Do you think getting expelled would tank your Stanford prospects?" Jackson asked. "That could mess with your head."

Xander was shaking his head even before Jackson finished. "It it might, and that could, but there just weren't any clues."

The barrista returned with the smoothie and latte. "You know, I think I made him the last turkey and avocado sandwich he ever had."

"He was here the night he died?" Xander asked.

"Yeah. Ordered a coke and a sandwich."

"Was he with anybody?"

The guy shook his dreads. "No. At least, not in line."

"Did you see him with anyone later?" Jackson asked.

"I don't know." He shrugged. "We got pretty busy."

"Thanks," Xander said lifting his latte.

As they walked away, a couple from the memorial came through the door. Jackson scanned the room then turned back toward the counter. "Did you see any suits that night?"

The rasta barrista looked at him blankly, still processing the order of the next person in line. "Suits?"

Jackson gestured with his chin toward the mourners filtering in.

"Ah, right." He turned his back to pull a shot of espresso from the machine behind him, dotted it with milk foam and turned back to deliver it to the woman waiting. "There weren't any events

Sunday, so it wasn't like this." The barrista looked off toward the back corner. "But now that you mention it, there was a guy. He didn't order anything, though." His focus shifted abruptly to the boys. "Why?"

"Uh . . .we don't want to take any more of your time," Jackson said, backing away.

"Yeah, we can see you're busy. Thanks, again," Xander added as he made a hasty exit.

Emily and Matthew were sitting close but not speaking when the boys quick-stepped over to the table. She looked even paler than before, if that were even possible.

"I can bring the car around," Xander offered again.

Emily shook her head. "No. I'm not even sure I want to go."

Jackson caught the look of panic in Xander's eyes and said, "None of us really wants to go, Emily, but we should do it. For his mom."

She nodded, and Xander started in the direction of the car so she wouldn't see his relieved smile.

Chapter 6

There was no parking to be found anywhere in College Terrace, so as with the memorial service, Xander dropped his brother and friends off and went on another quest for parking. He considered his strategy as he walked the three blocks back to TJ's house. Anybody smart enough to take TJ's body to the suicide crossing would never have left his phone untouched. What was he thinking even hoping he might get his hands on it? Even if it wasn't destroyed completely, any text and call threads linked to the killer would have been deleted for sure.

The Killer. That thought brought Xander up short. Not The Suit. The Killer. This wasn't just a puzzle to solve. He took a deep breath and started walking again. TJ deserved to have his name cleared and his killer brought to justice, and it didn't seem like anyone else was going to do it. They would just have to be careful. Xander straightened his tie as he jogged up the front steps. TJ's laptop was definitely the better bet, and he had a plan.

Jackson and Matthew were huddled in the corner behind the buffet with a bunch of other kids, inhaling cheese and crackers and looking vaguely uncomfortable. The rest of the dining room and living room were filled with adults in clusters and semicircles. The two rings nearest TJ's mom were somber and teary, listening to condolences and offering their own. The further from Mrs. Martin the adults were, the more animated the groups became, though they were still subdued. Xander scanned the room until he saw Emily waiting to speak to TJ's mom but hanging back deferring to the adults. He caught Jackson's eye and nodded toward Emily. Jackson nudged Matthew, and the two worked their way across the room until all three boys stood with Emily, shuffling in the condolence queue.

When their group reached the front, Emily said, "I'm so sorry!"

Then both women burst into tears and held each other in a tight hug.

Matthew's face flushed and he inspected his shoes. Jackson started to step back to give them privacy, but Xander grabbed his arm, holding him in place so they wouldn't lose the moment. Emily finally stepped back and wiped her face as TJ's mom dabbed at her eyes with the tissue clutched in her left hand.

"TJ was a great guy," Matthew said, shaking Mrs. Martin's hand. "He was always . . . he seemed so . . .," Matthew took a deep breath and started over. "I was lucky to know him."

Mrs. Martin smiled weakly. "Me, too."

Xander and Jackson introduced themselves and offered condolences, then Xander cleared his throat .

"Mrs. Martin . . . some of us were thinking that maybe we could turn TJ's facebook page into a memorial page? Make sure he's remembered for who he was, not how . . ." Having talked himself into a corner, he skipped ahead. "Would that be okay with you? We could do it on his computer right now, if you'd like."

She nodded. "That would be really nice. I know that's something he would have wanted, I just haven't had time to think about it. You don't need to do it now, though. I can give you his password."

"Thanks, Mrs. Martin." Xander threw a panicked look to Jackson as he pulled out his phone to make a note of the password.

"Would you mind if we took some pictures in his room? Some of his awards and things like that?" Jackson asked.

"Of course." She gestured toward the hallway. "Matthew can show you." She shook each of their hands again and gave Emily a brief squeeze before turning to the next group.

"You're welcome," Jackson muttered to Xander as they moved through the crowd .

"Yeah, that was good. Thanks."

Jackson looked over to see if Xander was being sarcastic, but he was completely focused on his phone as they followed Matthew. He smiled at the floor and nearly ran into Emily when she stopped abruptly at the start of the hall.

"I . . . I don't want to go. I'll just wait here."

"It's the second door on the left," Matthew said. "I think we'll go get something to drink and wait for you outside." He looked to Emily for confirmation, and she nodded.

"Hopefully this won't take long." Xander turned to Jackson and hurried him into the room. "Stand here and take a picture every now and then. Let me know if anyone is coming." He left Jackson

near the door and went directly to TJ's desk.

"What are you going to do?"

"Copy everything." Xander opened TJ's laptop, looked at

the screen, then pulled out the top drawer of the desk and started

rifling through it. He came up with an orange post it note. "Bingo!"

He typed in the password, and grinned. "Whatever changed for TJ

last weekend, our best shot at finding a clue is on his computer."

Xander pulled what looked like a royal blue cell phone out of his

pocket and plugged it into the computer.

"What is that?"

"Portable hard drive. I didn't want the hassle of multiple

flash drives."

"Sick." Jackson knew things like that existed, he just didn't

really care the way his brother did. He stepped back and scanned the

room with his phone, then took a few shots of the soccer trophies,

signed baseball, and music award that served as bookends on his

shelves. He picked up pieces to examine, periodically taking

photographs.

"Somebody's coming!" Jackson stepped backwards out the door, holding up his phone as Xander came around to the front of the desk and grabbed the first thing he could reach to pose for a photo.

"Oh, excuse me," a woman they didn't recognize said. "I'm looking for the restroom."

"No problem," Jackson said. "I think that's it." He pointed to the door across the hall. When the woman had gone inside and shut the door, he whispered, "A Python Manual? Really?"

Xander darted back around the desk to check the progress of the file transfer. He frowned, looked up at Jackson and picked up the manual he had tossed back onto the desk.

"Python . . . " he said to himself.

"What?"

"I'm not sure," Xander said, "but check out his book shelves. No other manuals, no books on technology, algorithms, anything remotely related to programming. This is almost as strange as the vodka in the locker."

The door across the hall opened and Jackson held up his phone, but the woman didn't even glance in. He checked the time. "How much longer?"

"Done!" Xander pocketed the drive and shut down the computer. He hesitated, picked up the Python manual, leafed through it and put it down next to the Woodhaven Handbook Matthew had delivered. "Let's go get Matthew and Emily."

They rode in silence to Emily's house. She got out at the curb, folding the seat forward so Jackson could climb out of the back and take her place. They exchanged a round of good-byes, then Emily retrieved her backpack and closed the trunk. She started to walk away, then leaned into the open passenger window.

"I think it's really nice what you're doing. The facebook memorial, I mean," she said in response to Xander's blank look.

Xander's thoughts had been on frame jobs and murder and programming, not on mourning, and he was chagrined in the face of Emily's sincere appreciation of his scam. "Thanks. I think it's the least we can do for TJ." He left off the rest of what he was thinking about how much more he intended to do. "Would you like to write the memorial statement for the page? You knew him better than we did."

Emily nodded. "I just couldn't talk about him, you know? At the service? I wanted to . . . but I could write something. I'll work on it right now."

As they pulled away from the curb, Matthew asked, "Did you find anything?"

"Maybe. Hard to say until I do a little more digging. Tell me about the last time you saw TJ." Xander met Matthew's eyes in the rearview mirror. "Were you in his room?"

Matthew nodded. "Yeah. I was only there for, like, ten minutes. He thanked me for the Handbook but just dumped it on his desk without even looking at it."

"Was he on his computer?"

"Course. He checked it a couple times while I was there." Matthew held up his hand. "Before you ask, I couldn't see the screen, so I don't know what he was doing."

Xander pulled into the driveway at Matthew's house and Jackson got out to fold down the passenger seat.

"Did TJ do much gaming?" Xander asked as Matthew extricated himself from the back seat.

Matthew shrugged. "As much as anybody. He played some online."

Xander popped the trunk. "What about design? Did he write apps?"

"Not that I ever heard." Matthew grabbed his backpack and closed the trunk. He walked back up to the driver's side window to exchange a hand slide fist bump with Xander. "Let me know if you need anything, okay?"

"Definitely."

As they pulled away from Matthew's house, a trumpet fanfare sounded from Xander's pocket.

"What the heck?" Jackson said.

Xander smiled broadly and stepped on the gas. "That, bro, means the recognition software just found a match."

Chapter 7

Xander drove home as fast as he could without triggering any police pursuit, and Jackson didn't even throw out a snappy comeback when Xander hurried to unlock the front door after popping the trunk shouting, "Grab my bag, too."

There was a note taped to the sliding glass door at the end of the atrium. Xander peeled it off as he walked in and carried it down the hallway to his room, reading as he walked. Jackson dumped the backpacks on the floor and followed in Xander's wake, leaving the door to the living room wide open.

"What is it?"

"Mom and Dad have a dinner in the City tonight. They're already gone. Money for pizza on the kitchen counter."

"Excellent!" Jackson pulled out his phone. "I'll order it now. The usual?"

"Yeah. And wings."

Xander fiddled with his laptop to see the recognition software hit while Jackson pulled up the Papa John's site and thumbed in their order for delivery. When he heard Xander snort, he looked up from the screen. "What?"

"Parker Compton."

Jackson screwed up his face. "What the heck? Is that a name or a law firm?"

"Look." Xander angled the screen so Jackson could see. "We should get Nicholas to confirm, but in the mean time, I can start looking for a connection to TJ."

"I don't think there's anybody named Compton at Woodhaven. Where's the photo from?"

"Could be a new kid . . . maybe a kid with a different last name," Xander said as he plugged the portable hard drive into his laptop. "This hit was from Linkedin. He's a partner at Digital Capital."

"Sandhill?"

"No duh! After TJ's files download, I'll have more to work with on the connection, but at least I can start trolling for data on our Mr. Compton." He went over to his bed, grabbed his iPad and yellow gamer glasses off the nightstand, and started sweeping his fingers across it as if conducting a tiny orchestra.

"Who gives their kid two last names, anyway? Parker Compton must be the whitest name ever. It's like the yacht racing of names."

"Fail!" Xander said, stopping his search to look up. "*Jackson Carter*? Really? Pot? Kettle? Glass house much? It's a WASP thing."

Jackson flushed, hating to be one-upped by his brother. "I *do* live in a glass house, and I can't be a WASP because I'm an atheist." He grinned. "I'm a WASA."

Xander shook his head and sighed as if the case were hopeless, then made a shooing gesture with one hand. "Go 'way. Call me when the pizza gets here. I'll send you a couple photos to forward to Nicholas. You can research Compton, too, if you want."

"No, thanks. I've got a Halo date." Jackson started to walk out of the room but paused in the doorway. "What about the facebook memorial?"

"Oh, right." Xander grimaced then went back to work. "I don't need to set that up until I hear from Emily. The site changes I need to make won't take very long."

Half an hour later, the doorbell rang. And rang again.

"Jax! Get the door!" Xander yelled from his room.

The doorbell rang again. Xander could hear it even with his earbuds in because his room was at the front of the house, so the ringing was extra annoying.

"Oh, my god, Jax! What are you, deaf?"

Xander stormed out of his room and through the open door to the atrium. He apologized to the pizza guy for taking so long, then had to go back inside for money. He tipped as his mother had taught him years before, then added a couple extra dollars because ever since his friend Ben started working in a pizza place, he knew how important tips were.

"Why didn't you get the door?" Xander said as he put the boxes on the kitchen counter.

"You just brought a ghost to a mantis fight, bro!"

Xander looked into the family room. Jackson was talking into a headset and involved in some epic battle with the television volume so high it was no wonder he couldn't hear the doorbell.

"What?" Jackson said.

Xander held up the box. "Pizza."

The boys moved around the kitchen in a self-service ballet, filling plates with pizza and grabbing paper towels.

"Soda?" Jackson asked.

"Nope," Xander said with his head inside the refrigerator. He came out with a gallon of milk and poured a glass.

Jackson replaced him at the refrigerator before the door could close and poured a glass of orange juice. They carried their plates and glasses into the family room where Jackson switched the television from game to the Tivo menu. He chose an episode of MadTV.

"Didn't we just see this one?" Xander asked.

Jackson shrugged without looking away from the screen and took a big bite of cheese pizza.

"I found a lot of stuff on Parker Compton," Xander said.

"Hello; watching this . . ." Jackson said, gesturing with his free hand.

Xander ate half a piece of pizza and continued. "He's got a daughter at St. Mark's, that's why we didn't recognize the name."

Jackson sighed and paused the program. "Fine. Just tell me."

"There was a Home volleyball game a few days before TJ was expelled."

"Against St. Mark's."

Xander nodded and chewed. "I think Compton and TJ must have met there."

"And what?"

"I don't know what! I 'm not clairvoyant. I'm just saying I can put them on campus at the same time."

"Dammit, Jim! I'm a hacker, not a mind-reader." Jackson smirked.

Xander rolled his eyes. "Ha. Ha. There was an ugly divorce that included charges of hiding assets, but they settled and sealed the record. Compton also faced an SEC investigation that was eventually dropped. Anyway, that's not the best part. When I went through TJ's recent files and applications, I found a PDF for an App Development Pitch contest for high school kids."

"Sponsored by Digital whatsis?"

"Exactly. And Compton's picture was on it. TJ was planning to enter that contest," Xander frowned, "though I can't imagine how. . . . but now it's our ticket to meet Parker Compton. I just have to come up with something before Tuesday's submission deadline. Ben's coming over after work to get started."

Jackson unpaused the TV. "Maybe you should get a job."

"Blog! Look who's talking. Testing video games is not a job."

"They pay me. How is that not a job? Besides, I'm not old enough to do anything else."

"Whatever," Xander said. "I had a *real* job."

"Yeah, 'had' being the operative word."

Xander went to the kitchen for more pizza and flopped back down on the couch. "Not my fault the library fired me."

Jackson raised one eyebrow at him and held the look.

"Well, not entirely. . . ." Xander started on another slice of pizza. "It's not my fault no one else could figure out how to access the files after I reorganized the desktop and streamlined the search system at tech support."

"Without permission," Jackson added.

"Taking initiative." Xander shrugged. "They should have thanked me."

Jackson shook his head. "What color is the sky in your world, bro?"

"How should I know?" Xander grinned. "I'm color blind."

It was past midnight when the front door opened and Mona and Dave Carter called out, "Hello, boys!"

"Hey, Mom, Dad," Jackson said from the family room.

"What are you watching?" Mona asked as she bent to kiss the top of his head.

"Movie. It's almost over. Stop!" He brushed away Dave's hand that was tousling his hair.

"Sorry. I'd hate to disturb your communion with the television."

"Good night, sweetie," Mona said. "Don't stay up too late."

"'Night. 'K."

The couple continued on to Xander's room where they heard voices behind the closed door. They could see Xander and Ben through the uncovered strip of window and knocked on the door.

"Sleepover?" Mona asked after Xander opened the door and the four had exchanged greetings.

"No, I was just about to go," Ben said. He grabbed his keys from the book shelf and turned to Xander as he exited. "See ya tomorrow."

"How was dinner?" Xander asked his parents.

"Great!" Mona said.

"It was worth the drive to get to spend a few hours with the Bronks while they were in town," Dave added.

"We thought about staying over," Mona said.

"Why didn't you? Oh, wait, let me guess . . . Dad has work to do?"

"Everybody's a critic," Dave said. "But yes. See you in the morning."

Xander turned his attention back to his computer after his parents left, closing the window with the app notes and opening TJ's memorial facebook page. He had hoped that Emily wouldn't get the statement to him until the next day, but when her email arrived around ten, he had felt obligated to take care of the post right away. Ben had arrived not long after, so there were still a few tweaks that needed to be made. Xander was surprised to see how much traffic the site had already. He scrolled through the comments and memories and good thoughts until one caught his eye.

It didn't have to end this way. You should have come to see me again.

Xander looked at the signature, then pulled up the window with TJ's hard drive on it and systematically searched every file opened in the two weeks before TJ was expelled.

"Oh my god . . . "

He ran to his door and threw it open. "Jax!"

A muffled "What?" came from the bathroom.

"Everything okay, boys?" Dave Carter called from the office.

"Yes, Dad." Xander responded.

He walked over to the bathroom door and spoke just above a whisper. "Come to my room as soon as you're done."

When Jackson walked into the room, Xander was sitting facing the door with one knee jiggling up and down. "What?" Jackson asked.

Xander lifted his chin toward the door and waited while Jackson closed it. "Look at this." He pointed to the email exchange open on the screen. "I found someone else who met with TJ last week."

Jackson's eyes grew wide as he read the email. He looked at Xander, then read the messages again.

Please don't speak to anyone until you give me a chance to explain. It really isn't what you think, but I can't afford to have anyone know.

Give me a reason not to report you.

I can make it worth your while.

I'll come to the lab.

We should meet off campus.

The signature line for the messages not from TJ was the Woodhaven standard faculty response for Julie Warner.

"This is TJ with Dr. Warner, the chemistry teacher?" Jackson asked.

Xander nodded. "Yeah. Last week."

"Do you think it was . . ." Jackson hesitated, " blackmail?"

"I don't know what was going on between the two of them, but we need to find out. Could be we just found someone else who had a reason to hurt TJ."

Chapter 8

"USB tether!" Xander said as he brushed past Jackson in the hall Saturday afternoon.

"What?"

"Nothing." He made a dismissive gesture. "Ben needs to share . . . be right back - gotta restart the router. Different thing."

"Blog." Jackson heard the garage door slam as he walked into Xander's room shaking his head. All the computer support equipment was housed in the same space as their mom's studio. Fortunately, Xander's occasional dashing in and out didn't bother her. Jackson leaned against the bookshelf across from where Ben was sitting on the bed working on a laptop.

"Hey, Jax."

Jackson lifted his chin. "You guys got anything?"

Ben wrinkled his nose as if something nearby smelled bad.

"Kinda. I wanted to go with his first idea, the Pigs for Peace game where you send pigs into battle zones and get bacon when they explode, but Xander thinks the psych game is the way to go."

"What's the psych game?

"Glad you asked," Xander said as he ran back into the room and entered data into his laptop. "Okay, everything should be back up." He turned around. "You know the Myers-Briggs personality test?"

Jackson squinted. "A bunch of letters on some scale? Introvert/Extrovert, that one?"

"Yeah. A lot of companies use it as a tool for putting together work teams and even for hiring sometimes."

Jackson shrugged. "So?"

Xander smiled broadly. "So what if there were a game where your actions corresponded to questionnaire responses? As you play, you develop the profile. The HR manager could encourage interviewees to try it out while waiting. It would look like a fun way to pass the time before the interview, but in reality, it would be part of the interview! Sick, huh?"

"Um, yeah . . .," Jackson said. "but not the way you mean. More like creepy."

Ben threw up his hands. "That's what I said!"

"Hey, it may be creepy, but it'll get us a slot. We should be able to set it up on our Minecraft server so we can control the options. If we can get even three questions for each category, that will be enough for the pitch demo."

"Loner."

"Look who's talking. What about Dr. Warner? Anything?"

Jackson blew a curl off his forehead. "Well, there weren't any more email exchanges besides the one you found. Whatever discussions they had must have been in person."

"Which is pretty sketchy," Ben said.

Jackson gave him a Spock brow. "Talking in person is not a crime."

"No, but it's not normal, either."

"Anyway," Jackson continued, "I did find two interesting things. TJ had a file on west Texas acacia plants opened the same week as that email you found."

Xander had already lost interest and turned back to his keyboard. "So?"

"So it also had a bunch of stuff about pseudophedrine and anhydrous ammonia."

Xander spun around, eyes wide. "No way!"

Jackson nodded and smiled. "Yes way."

"What?" Ben asked.

"So TJ thought Dr. W was all Breaking Bad?" Xander ran one hand through his hair while the other looked like it was typing on his knee. "But what the heck is the acacia about? Isn't that pink shrub in the back yard an acacia?"

"Don't ask me, dude." Jackson held up his hands in surrender. "Just telling you what I found. Weird though, right?"

"What? What?" Ben asked, looking back and forth between the brothers.

"Looks like maybe TJ thought Dr. Warner was cooking meth," Xander said.

Ben's jaw dropped. "Fail! That's just crazy!"

"True. But at least we know what to look for when we get to the lab and talk to her." Xander shifted back to face the desk. "Okay, let's get back to the app. We need a decent demo if we want to get in to meet Mr. Compton."

"Can we take a food break?" Ben asked. "I'm starving."

Xander waved him away. "I'm sure there's something in the fridge."

"C'mon," Jackson said. "I was going to get some cold pizza before I go to Josh's."

"I'm not giving you a ride," Xander said without turning around.

"No duh. I'm riding my bike. Next year I'll be able to drive."

"Not my car."

Jackson snorted. "I don't think 'car' is the noun you're looking for," as he walked out he added, "'baby' would be closer."

Late that night Xander heard Jackson get home from the Giants game, talk with their parents, then head to his room. An IM window popped up on his screen within seconds of Jackson's door closing.

skype

Xander logged in and Jackson's face appeared on the laptop.

"Josh's mom knows Dr. Warner!"

"So do we. What's your point?"

"No, I mean they're friends. Josh's mom talked about her tonight at the game."

Xander perked up at that. "Really?"

"Yeah. Apparently TJ's death hit her really hard." Jackson paused for effect. "Especially because her dad *in Missouri* is in some expensive hospice place."

A door closed somewhere in the house and both boys were silent.

"So Dr. Warner's from Missouri?"

"Yeah," Jackson said. "And she's been going to visit two or three weekends every month since her dad got sick."

"Did you say anything to Josh's mom about Missouri being the meth capital of the midwest?"

Jackson rolled his eyes. "That is not exactly an appropriate comment in the middle of a conversation about grieving. Besides, until today, we didn't know that, either."

"So 'No' then?"

"Ya think?"

"Propriety is overrated." Xander chewed on a hangnail. "That it?"

"No. I heard back from Nicholas. Apparently the file you gave me to forward had a bunch of different pictures?"

"Yeah. I decided to give him multiple choice to see if he could really ID the guy. What'd he say?"

"Certainty isn't really his strong suit, but Compton was his first choice."

Xander nodded. "Good enough for now. 'Night."

"One more thing," Jackson said. "What've you got to do tomorrow?"

"Finish the app and submit it before the deadline."

"Do the app ap?" Jackson grinned.

Xander didn't acknowledge the lame attempt at humor. "And homework. Why?"

"Because I'm pretty sure I left a book in the Physics lab on Friday."

"So what . . ." Xander stopped when he realized where Jackson was going and frowned. "So Dr. Warner shares the lab. The classrooms are locked on Sundays."

"But the cleaning crew is there." Jackson smiled. "You know Chica will let me in."

The boys stood in the middle of the lab trying to decide where to begin. The place looked pristine.

"Locked cabinets, maybe?" Jackson said.

Xander shook his head. "Put these on." He pulled some latex gloves out of his pocket and handed them to Jackson then put some on himself.

"What the heck?"

"Mom keeps them in the studio. If we do find anything related to meth, we for sure don't want our fingerprints on it."

"Good point."

"You take those cabinets; I'll start with the desk."

The brothers worked fast, rifling every cupboard, drawer and shelf, coming up empty every time.

Xander peeled off his gloves. "If TJ did see something, Dr. Warner must have gotten rid of it by now."

The door opened and the boys spun to face it.

"Todo bien?" Chica asked. "Did you find your book, Jax."

Jackson shoved his gloved hands into his pockets, shaking his head dejectedly. "No, Chica. Maybe it wasn't here." He brightened suddenly. "Wait! Maybe it's in the cabinet. Doesn't Dr. Warner put her lost and found in there?" He looked at Xander with his eyebrows raised.

"Yeah . . . .that's right. Mostly for phones or iPads, but she might put textbooks there, too."

"Let me see if I can help," Chica flipped through the ring of keys at her waist, coming up with a tiny silver one that fit the cabinet. Xander nodded to Jackson and tilted his head to the left as she opened both doors wide.

The three crowded in front of the shelves, with Xander scanning the right side as fast as he could and Jackson the left.

"I don't see a book. Lo siento, Jax." Chica closed and locked the cabinet and turned to walk out with the boys, locking the lab behind them.

"Gracias, Chica. No problem. I'll check in the office tomorrow."

The boys didn't say anything until they got in the car.

"Jar with a Texas address," Jackson said, "it was labeled A berlandieri. Maybe that's some kind of acacia?"

Xander smiled. "Big bottle of small red pills labeled 'sucrose' way down on the bottom shelf."

"Sucrose?"

"Yeah. Totally plausible, but it sure looked like Sudafed to me."

Chapter 9

"So what's the plan with Dr. Warner?" Jackson asked on the drive to school Monday morning. He continued thumbing the game on his phone without looking up.

Xander shook his head. His eyes were red-rimmed and only half open. It had been a long night. He had spent hours on his ap, trying to figure out game actions that would correlate to Meyers-Briggs (You hear a group on the other side of the trees, do you approach them or go around?) and then went back through TJs Nike+ records to see if he had checked in anywhere or had a shift in his activity pattern in the days after the email exchange with Dr. Warner.

"I don't know. Ask me tomorrow. I've got journalism after school and the app has to be in by noon to reserve a pitch spot."

Jackson shrugged. "'K. I'll come to the library after practice. I can get a ride with Josh if you're not done."

"Something's not right with the whole Dr. Warner thing, though," Xander said after a few minutes.

"Like how would one of our teachers end up cooking meth?" Jackson spared a quick sideways glance from his game.

"No. I mean why would she leave anything incriminating in the lab if TJ had already confronted her?"

"Um . . . hubris?"

"Really? Hubris? Loner!"

Jackson smirked to himself, then said. "So we're missing something."

"We're missing a lot . . . but I just don't have the bandwidth to think about it right now. The time between TJ's email exchange with Dr. Warner and that last check in from the Coho doesn't show anything unusual."

"Maybe there shouldn't be," Jackson said. "If TJ picked the meeting spot, he would choose someplace familiar."

Xander pulled into a parking spot and looked over at Jackson. "Sometimes you are not a total idiot."

The talk around the Junior lunch table where Xander's friends sat was pretty subdued. Most of them had Writing after lunch, and the rough draft for their personal essay was due. Xander had propped his iPad in the portable keyboard and was typing furiously between bites of a tuna on sourdough.

"Sorry to interrupt . . .," Emily appeared beside him.

Xander looked up, irritated at the interruption, but when he saw who it was, he managed a small smile. She did get him into TJ's house, after all. "No, it's okay." He forced himself not to glance at the screen.

"I wanted to ask you a favor." She started to tear up, and looked past him, blinking hard.

In a mild panic, Xander looked from one of his friends to the next, but they were all engrossed in their computers. He took a deep breath and stood up, walking Emily a little way away from the table. "Are you okay?"

She continued to stare past him to the tree-studded hills beyond the field. "It's such a beautiful day, don't you think? It doesn't seem right that it should be so perfect even after . . ."

Xander followed her gaze. The sky was a bright blue, the trees were winter green. It was just a regular day.

Emily continued as if she'd heard his thoughts. "But it's always beautiful, right? Oh, there's a little rain, there are a few hot days, but we're spoiled. Maybe just living here makes you spoiled. TJ wasn't, though. He didn't take things for granted, ever. He worked for everything and had big plans."

Her tears had dried and her voice had hardened as she spoke. Xander looked longingly at his iPad and involuntarily cleared his throat. The sound seemed to shake Emily out of her developing rant.

"Sorry. Um . . .yeah. They asked me if I would write about TJ for the school paper . . . and I was hoping you might be able to do something with what I gave you for the Facebook memorial." She looked at the ground and shook her head slightly. "I just can't do another one."

"You know I'm just the Webmaster, right? I don't really do content . . ." he saw Emily's face start to crumple as she looked up at him. " . . . but I'm sure we can make something work from the Facebook memorial."

"Thanks, Xander; you're the best!" She rose on her tiptoes to kiss him on the cheek before leaving.

Xander started typing again before his behind even hit the bench.

"Oooh, Xander! You're the best!" Ben led the group at the table in a falsetto chorus.

Xander gave them a finger without looking up. He copied the end of his outline, pasted it into his rough draft, and started filling in sentences between the points. It was his best bet for getting a passable version in time for class. The bell rang, and he didn't stand, still typing. The rest of the group packed up.

"You coming?" Reza asked.

"C'mon," Ben said to Reza. "He'll make it."

"I've got an idea about Dr. Warner." Jackson had split off from his friends heading to class to stop beside Xander.

Xander ignored him as he typed a few rapid-fire sentences, then shut everything down and swept it into his backpack. He crammed the last of his sandwich into his mouth and dumped the plate in the trash.

"Mrrf," he said, gesturing down the walkway.

Jackson grimaced in exaggerated disgust. "Nice."

"What do you want?" Xander managed as he chewed.

"Lemme try it first. I'll tell you later."

Xander shrugged. "Whatever."

During the afternoon break Jackson lingered by the drinking fountain next to the science lab. When Dr. Warner left the lab, he bent quickly to take a drink, then stood up as she passed him.

"Dr. Warner!"

The tall brunette turned.

"I just wanted you to know I saw you at TJ's memorial. It was really nice of you to come . . . not many teachers did."

She brushed a strand of hair behind her hair and cleared her throat. "Thank you for saying so."

"TJ must have thought a lot of you," Jackson said. "He told us he was going to work with you on a special project."

Jackson watched the chemistry teacher closely. Her eyes widened and her mouth dropped open for a fraction of a second before she rearranged her face and frowned slightly. It was just the sort of reaction he had been hoping to see.

"Really?" She shook her head slowly. "His death was . . . unnecessary. TJ had many gifts." She hesitated and looked past him before continuing. "What did he have to say about his . . . project?"

The bell rang on schedule and Jackson backed up toward the gym. "Sorry . . . class. Thanks, again, for showing up for TJ." He turned and walked the opposite way down the walkway, smiling to himself, resisting the temptation to look back over his shoulder.

Half an hour later, his self-control was rewarded. A senior appeared beside the PE teacher with a note, and the teacher waved Jackson off the field.

"Kolton! Go in for Jax."

Jackson jogged over to Mr. Moore and accepted the folded paper with "Jackson Carter" written on the outside. The note read:

Please see me at your earliest convenience. I have office hours after school all this week.

The signature was Dr. Warner's.

Chapter 10

"But I have a game today!" Jackson protested after spitting out toothpaste. "And what about Dr. Warner?"

"Sorry," Xander said. "The contest was designed to be intentionally high stress. The pitches are all scheduled for the next three days by random assignment. We either make the slot we were given this afternoon or we're out."

"Are you even ready for this?" Jackson wiped his mouth and stuffed the white-smeared hand towel onto the bar.

"I was born ready."

Jackson met Xander's eyes in the mirror with a withering stare. "Seriously?"

Xander shrugged. "Okay, I could have used a little more time, but . . ."

He was cut off by a call from the living room.

"Boys? Is this a school holiday I didn't know about?"

The boys grabbed their backpacks and bolted through the living room and out the sliding glass door to the atrium.

"Thanks, Mom," Jackson yelled.

"We've got a presentation after school, so we'll be late," Xander added.

"Have a great day!" Mona yelled at their backs, shaking her head at the over the shoulder backwards wave both offered after they'd passed her.

Xander backed out and took off for school slightly faster than the posted limit. "I'm ready enough," he continued as they drove. "I blew off my Spanish homework."

"Dude, you can't get detention today."

"Relax, Jax, I can get it done at lunch. It doesn't have to be good, just finished."

Jackson frowned. "Um . . . don't you have this little thing called college applications to worry about? You know, grades?"

Xander waved him off. "I'll be fine."

Jackson was delayed in his last class and had to run to the parking lot, hoping that he hadn't left anything in his locker. He'd shown his coach the contest flyer at lunch time so he wouldn't have any issues on that front, but his Lit teacher seemed constitutionally incapable of stopping a monologue mid-thought, bell or no bell. As he dashed past the science lab, he waved and smiled at Dr. Warner.

Ben was standing beside the passenger door with the seat up for Jackson to climb into the back and Xander had the engine running when he got to the car. Ben was wearing a button-down shirt and khaki pants, a far cry from his usual jeans and obscure graphic t-shirt. Jackson tossed his backpack in and squeezed past the seat. Xander started backing up as soon as Ben closed the door.

"Are you wearing . . . a suit?" Jackson asked, finally settling in enough to actually look at his brother.

"Duh!"

"But I thought the lawyers and money guys wore the suits and the nerds wore T-shirts and polos."

Xander glanced into the rearview mirror to meet Jackson's eyes. "I need the jacket. I'll take it off as soon as we get there, roll up the sleeves on the shirt. Trust me; I have a plan."

"Speaking of which," Ben said, "what the heck is it?"

Xander turned off the winding hill road that ran past Woodhaven and onto the four lane street that would take them to the freeway. "We go in, run our demo, make the pitch, and respond to questions just like anybody else. At the very least, we'll get to see Parker Compton up close and see if he reacts when we mention Woodhaven."

"And at the most?" Jackson asked.

"I'm going to try to bump his phone. That's what the jacket is for, so I can pop my phone out of the pocket while I'm folding the jacket."

"Fail!" Jackson said. "What are the odds you're going to get anywhere near his phone?"

"I don't know, but in every picture I found of this guy except his LinkedIn profile, he was holding a phone. I'll bet he has it out on the table or in his hand at some point before or after our pitch."

Jackson shook his head. "If you didn't already owe me money, I might take that bet."

"He may be right," Ben added. "The guys who eat in at Pizza My Mind pretty much never look away from their phones, even the suits. They're even worse than girls!"

"Fine, I'll buy that it's plausible. But how do you know he'll have bump, too?"

Xander shrugged. "Who doesn't?"

Ben nodded in agreement and leaned around the seat to look at Jackson. "Those venture guys clink their phones so often you'd think they had champagne."

"Nice!" Xander offered a casual fist bump without taking his eyes off the road.

Jackson snorted. "Like you'd know from champagne. Okay, fine, I give up. But why am *I* here?" Jackson asked.

"I ask myself that everyday," Xander said.

Ben snickered.

"Lone! Seriously."

"Because you're going to go to the men's room after our intro."

"I can pee here if you pull over," Jackson said.

Ben and Jackson both looked at Xander, waiting for the real explanation.

"While Ben and I make the pitch to the panel, you're going to visit Compton's office. The restrooms should be past his office and around the corner from the conference room where the presentations are being held."

"And you know this because . . . . " Ben said.

"Blueprints filed with the city for a remodel two years ago and a photo series from a profile Wired did on Compton."

Ben shook his head. "You don't ever sleep, do you?"

"Google never sleeps, " Xander said. "but I do okay."

Jackson sighed. "I hesitate to ask, but what, exactly, am I going to do in Compton's office, assuming I can get in."

Xander reached into his pocket and held a folded tissue over his right shoulder for Jackson to take. "There's a wireless dongle in there. If there's a lap top, put it into an open USB port. If there's a desk top, put it in the keyboard." When Jackson didn't immediately take the kleenex from him, Xander shook it and looked into the rearview mirror. "Jax!"

"I'm pretty sure wiretapping is illegal," Jackson said.

"It's not wiretapping!"

"Corporate espionage, then?"

"Look," Xander said, "you may not have a chance to do anything at all, anyway, but it could be our chance to connect him to TJ."

Jackson reluctantly took the tissue and stuffed it into his own pocket. "I assume you cleaned it and the kleenex is to keep it print-free?"

"No-duh!" Xander said as he took the Sandhill exit and turned toward the Digital Capital.

The boys were silent for the few minutes it took to find the address, pull into the lot and park. After Ben climbed out, Jackson pushed the seat up with his feet to get out of the back.

"Feet off the seat!" Xander glared at Jackson.

"Okay, let's make sure we have everything," Xander said as they unloaded their backpacks and Ben checked the equipment. "Jax, don't leave the room until after we introduce ourselves so you can watch Compton's reaction, okay?"

Jackson had the sort of butterflies he got before going on stage. "Okay."

"Here," Xander said, "take this, too." He handed a silver iPod nano to Jackson. "Leave that in the restroom or drop it behind something in the hallway. Just in case we need an excuse to get back in."

Jackson nodded, shoved it into his other pocket, and slammed the passenger door. Xander shouldered his backpack and started toward the lobby entrance, patting first one jacket pocket then the other.

Jackson swallowed hard and took a deep breath. "You ready, Ben?"

Ben shook his head but started after Xander. "I think I'm going to be sick."

Chapter 11

"Touring Napa - Xander Carter and Ben Norton?"

The boys stood when the man opened the door and announced their project. The group before them had looked a little shaken when they'd walked out about ten minutes before, and Ben was very pale.

"Breathe!" Xander said quietly out of the side of his mouth.

They followed the man into the room and shook hands all around. There were two other men on the panel, including Parker Compton. Compton's phone was in his hand, but he put it down as they walked in. Jackson handed things to Ben in order to look useful during the set up, then moved back against the wall near the door and with a good view of Compton. Before Xander began, he leaned over to the man who had called the group in and asked about the men's room.

"Good afternoon," Xander began. "I'm Xander Carter and this is Ben Norton. We're here from Woodhaven High with a game that can determine the Myers-Briggs personality type of the player though the choices made and can therefore be used as a human resources tool for work groups and companies of any size."

Jackson watched Compton during the intro. Initially he looked bored, his eyes on the presentation but his hand on his phone. At the mention of Woodhaven, his eyes darted sideways to his colleagues then narrowed and focused more intently on Xander. His face flushed and he touched his collar, but then he remained perfectly still. Not exactly an admission of guilt, but definitely a reaction.

"The easiest of the four dimensions to measure is Introvert/Extrovert. By counting the number of conversations initiated, length of conversations, and alliances formed . . ." Jackson backed out the door as Xander spoke, holding it so it would close silently.

He heard voices in the lobby, probably the next group arriving, and turned to walk in the opposite direction hoping to get to Compton's office before they saw him. The name plate appeared on the wall just about where Xander had predicted, and Jackson walked in, scanning the room and clutching the tissue in his pocket. His heart was pounding as he crossed to the desk.

No laptop visible and he wasn't going to go through the drawers to find one, but there was a computer on the desk. He pulled his hand out of his pocket and peeled back the kleenex to expose the dongle, but his phone began to vibrate and startled him so much he dropped the tiny black rectangle on the desk. Jackson closed his eyes, took a deep breath, then picked up the device and shoved it into the USB port on the keyboard. He used the tissue to wipe it off and hurried out of the room.

Jackson walked around the corner to the men's room and leaned against the wall as soon as the door closed behind him. He splashed some cold water on his face, dried it off, and put the nano face down on top of the paper towel dispenser where it would blend in. He cursed Xander under his breath for getting him involved in this crazy scheme, then walked back to the conference room. Two boys and a girl sat on the bench seat outside the room straining to hear the muffled voices inside. Jackson gave them a chin lift and slipped into the room as silently as possible.

"With full disclosure the liability and privacy concerns should be fully addressed," Xander was saying as Jackson stepped to the back of the room. Jackson gave a slight nod to show he'd accomplished his mission.

Ben and Xander now looked exactly like the team that had walked out before them, somewhere between carsick and roadkill. The Q and A sounded more like the inquisition than the kind of project critique and feedback they were used to at school. Jackson watched the panel as they peppered Xander with questions. Leaning back, glancing at their phones, they were already done. He shifted slightly to catch Ben's eye, which wasn't hard to do since Ben was trying to look anywhere but at the panel. Jackson pushed his nose up with one finger and raised his eyebrows. Ben frowned, and Jackson nodded his head repeatedly.

Xander caught the exchange. He cleared his throat.

"Of course, if you prefer games with no purpose beyond entertainment that are simple enough to play on your phone, we have something else." He reached in front of Ben to open a new file. Ben smiled a little grimly as he caught on and started the demo.

"In a fictional war zone, many land mines have been left behind. In order to make the place habitable again, the humanitarian organization Pigs for Peace goes in with livestock to detonate the mines." On the screen a pig exploded into bacon, and Compton laughed.

Xander and Ben wrapped up the presentation with the few minutes they had left, packed up, and shook hands all around, thanking the men for their time and the contest. When he got to Parker Compton, Xander angled his left side in close as he offered his hand.

"You know nobody changes direction mid-presentation, right" Compton's eyes were dark and shiny, like the glass beads used in taxidermy .

"Well . . .," Xander glanced over at Ben and Jackson, "my friend TJ said you might be flexible."

Compton's grip tightened until it was uncomfortable, but Xander didn't flinch. "Did he?"

Xander managed a nod but couldn't speak or break eye contact.

After a moment Compton lifted one corner of his mouth and let go. "See you soon, I'm sure."

All three boys filed out. No one spoke until they had left the building.

"Oh my god! That was the worst . . ."

Before Ben could continue, Xander cut him off. "Not yet. Take this stuff." He handed his jacket to Ben and put the bag on the ground at his feet, then turned to Jackson and shoved him.

"What the dump?"

"Shove me back."

Jackson did not have to be invited twice.

Xander ruffled Jackson's hair with both hands. "Now chase me!" he said, taking off across the lawn. When Jackson didn't follow, Xander turned around, jogging backwards and making taunting gestures.

Ben and Jackson exchanged a look.

"Do you think he's lost it?" Ben asked.

"I've always thought that."

"Loooooooner!" Xander yelled.

Jackson sighed. "I guess we'll never know unless I run down there."

When Jackson got close, Xander started running again, then stumbled, crashing into Jackson and sending them both through the shrubs and up against the building. Xander stood up laughing, then leaned against the building to catch his breath. He offered a hand to Jackson, which Jackson eyed suspiciously before pulling himself up.

"Let's go," Xander said.

Jackson shook his head and brushed plant debris off his pants as he walked.

"Ummm . . . are you okay?" Ben asked as Xander collected his belongings and they all moved toward the car. "I mean, that was pretty much the worst experience of my entire life, but still . . ."

"You mean other than being verbally eviscerated by the gang of three and then having Compton look at me like a leopard gecko looking at a cricket? Yeah, I'm fine. That show was for the security cameras. I needed to plant a signal amplifier on Compton's window so I can access the dongle from the parking lot."

Jackson shook his head. "Okay, even if he doesn't notice the little black bit in the keyboard right away, don't you think someone is going to notice some kind of amplifier stuck to the window?"

Xander smiled. "No. You know why?" He reached into the pocket of his jacket. "Check out my back up." He held out his hand to reveal what looked like a large garden spider.

Jackson leaned in. On closer inspection, the spider was a little beat up, and the pattern on the body was circuitry.

Xander smiled. "I told you before, it's not a bug - it's a spider!"

Chapter 12

"Fail! Where the heck did you get that thing?" Jackson climbed into the backseat and Ben popped the passenger seat back up and dropped into it like a lead weight.

"Hey! Fold the seat back down, loner. My foot's stuck."

"Sorry, Jax."

Ben leaned forward enough to angle the seat and Jackson wiggled his foot out from being pinned against the door.

Xander started the car. "If you two are finished . . . ," He glanced at Jackson in the rearview mirror as he drove away from Digital Capital. "Remember that friend of Dad's who worked on drones?"

"Yeah . . . "

"Don't you remember that story he had about the CIA using fake dragonflies to bug people?"

"No pun intended." Jackson smirked.

Xander ignored him. "I thought a spider would be better. No one would notice if it hung in one spot for awhile."

"Please tell me you didn't use a real spider," Ben said.

"I tried, but even shellacked it just wasn't stable enough."

Jackson made a fake gagging sound into his hands.

"The nature store had some pretty realistic plastic ones, though, with room in the back to hollow out for the signal booster."

"Sick!" Ben said.

Jackson rubbed his eyes and pulled out his phone and started checking messages. "I'm just glad that's over."

"For you, maybe," Xander said. "There are pitch sessions scheduled until 8:00. I'm going to be in the parking lot when Compton gets back to his desk."

"Looks like not seeing Dr. Warner today wasn't such a bad thing after all," Jackson said. "She'll be waiting for me in the science lab at lunch period tomorrow." He looked into the rearview mirror. "Maybe you should come, too."

Xander met his eyes. "Yeah, maybe I should."

"How was your presentation today?" Mona asked as she passed the pistachio-crusted chicken to Jackson.

"What kind of presentation?" Dave asked.

Jackson forked a hunk of chicken into his mouth and held up a finger while he chewed to buy some time. Xander's plan to hack Compton's computer clearly hadn't included the possibility that their parents would both be home for dinner and hoping for quality time. Or maybe tossing Jackson to the wolves was the plan all along.

"It wasn't my presentation," he said, "I was just helping Xander and Ben."

Mona frowned. "This wasn't what you needed the facial recognition for app for?"

"Facial recognition?" Dave raised his eyebrows. "What did you need that for, Jax?"

Jackson chewed his next bite really well, silently cursing Xander each time his teeth met.

"This wasn't our school project, this was that app pitch thing that Ben and Xander worked on over the weekend. It went . . . okay, I guess. The second app got a decent response.

"They changed their pitch halfway through?" Dave shook his head.

"Why?" Mona asked.

"Parker Compton told Xander nobody does that," Jackson answered.

Dave Carter stopped eating. "Parker Compton was there?"

"Well . . . yeah." Jackson scanned his father's face for some indication of what he should say next. Something was off, but Jackson didn't know why. "Digital Capital sponsored the contest."

"What's the prize?"

Jackson was thrown off by the intensity of the interest and continued hesitantly. "The top three get tested with focus groups . . . and then the winner gets $1000 and support for production of the game."

Dave shook his head and started eating again. "Well, that sounds like a great PR stunt and fine way to troll for fresh ideas. Just be careful getting involved with Parker Compton."

The expression on his father's face told Jackson they'd entered "I could tell you, but then I'd have to kill you" territory, so he didn't ask why.

At 8:05 Xander turned into Digital Capital and parked in a spot near enough to the few other cars there so he wouldn't draw attention. He backed in in case he needed to make a quick exit, cut his engine, and fired up his laptop.

"C'mon, Compton . . . check your mail."

Not getting a phone bump after the meeting had been disappointing. Xander was pretty sure that TJ would have been texting whoever he met before he died, but getting Compton's phone data had been a long shot. There could have been e-mail, though. Compton was too old to choose text over email, even using his phone.

"Yes!"

Xander's typing sounded like a submachine gun in a video game. He sent code to access existing data and began the download. He watched as the completion percentage bar filled up. When it finished, he immediately began entering the code to enable later remote access. A movement in the side mirror caught his eye. The security guard was heading right for him! Xander dumped the laptop onto the passenger seat, started the car and squealed out of the parking lot.

He took Sandhill away from 280, heading for Foothill Expressway, instead. He drove fast for a short distance, then slowed and changed lanes to fall between two trucks, checking his mirrors all the way home. Even when he turned onto his own street, he drove around the corner and parked for five minutes, just in case. Finally, he pulled up in front of the house, gathered his things and went in.

"Hi, Sweetie!" Mona called from the family room.

"Hey, Mom!" Xander called back. He headed directly for his room to see if he'd gotten anything useful from his brief connection.

Xander dropped his backpack, grabbed his glasses and plugged in his laptop. Jackson appeared in the doorway before he had time to do more than power it up.

"Well?"

"Gimme a minute."

While Xander scrolled and typed and read the screen, Jackson stepped into the room and closed the door.

"Dad said to be careful getting involved with Compton," Jackson blurted out.

Xander looked up. "What? What did you tell him?"

"Nothing! I was just answering questions *at dinner* about the contest. I'm just sayin' . . . Dad knows something about him."

Xander hmmphed and returned his attention to the screen. "Nothing from TJ . . . nothing that looks weird, lots of memos and proposals," Xander said as he checked the files he was able to download. "Let me see if I have the recently deleted emails . . ."

Xander stopped typing abruptly, maybe stopped breathing. He stared at the screen.

"What? What?" Jackson demanded.

Xander looked up at Jackson. The pale blue light of the screen combined with the yellow tint of the gamer glasses to turn his face a sickly gray-green. "The last new mail in Compton's in box was my license plate number."

Chapter 13

"What the frick?"

"The security guard must have sent it just before I spotted him and abandoned the parking lot."

"But why?"

Xander ran his fingers through his hair. "I don't know. Maybe they're paranoid. Or maybe they just wanted to be sure none of the applicants was waiting around to try to chat with the panel. I just wish I'd had time to learn a little more about him before I showed up on his radar."

"What about the TJ comment after the pitch?"

"Exactly. I wanted him to start wondering about me, not be sure I'm a problem."

Jackson pursed his lips as he thought, then snapped his fingers. "The nano!"

"The last thing I need is another trip to Digital Capital. Lone!"

"Ranger! You call tomorrow, tell them when you came back to look for the nano, it was obvious the building was closed." He smiled and held his hands out palms up. "Suspicion diffused."

Xander frowned and nodded slowly. "That could work. And as long as I don't pick it up, it still provides the excuse to go back." He spun around to face the desk, making a shooing gesture with his hand as he turned. "I need to get back to work."

"Are you coming with me to see Dr. Warner tomorrow?" Jackson asked before he left.

Without breaking the rhythm of his clicking keys, Xander said, "I'll be there."

"Ow!" Xander said in response to the gentle hand on his ankle.

"Really, loner?" Jackson said. "Get up already."

Xander threw his feet over the edge of the bed and sat up without opening his eyes.

"Did you sleep with you computer?"

"Maybe."

"Fail!" Jackson said. "Too bad you can't move your phone and computer out to your car and sleep there. Then your life would be perfect."

"Troll," Xander mumbled.

Xander dragged himself through getting dressed and packing up his school things while Jackson leaned in the doorway texting his friends.

"Do you mind?" Xander asked in a voice dripping with sarcasm.

"No, not at all." Jackson smirked.

"'Bye Mom, 'Bye Dad!" they yelled as they jostled out the sliding glass door and through the front door to the car.

They drove to school in silence, Jackson flipping through messages on his phone and jumping from screen to screen, Xander doing something pretty much the same in his brain. At the last turn approaching Woodhaven, he said, "There's something screwy about Parker Compton."

"What?" Jackson asked automatically. When the statement registered he said, "No duh."

Xander frowned and drummed his fingers on the wheel. "There are gaps in some if his mail threads . . . like the exchange was altered but not deleted."

"Exchanges with TJ?"

"No, with some guy at a company called TSC. TranStemCo."

"What's that, the most generic company name they could come up with?" Jackson asked.

Xander shrugged. "All the good names are taken. Either you name your company after yourself or you put the words trans, gen, matrix, co, pro, stem, meta, and ware on some dice and roll them until you get one you like that doesn't turn up on a search." He pulled into the school lot and parked in his usual spot. "The emails didn't seem all that strange, but the glitchy bits start a couple weeks before TJ got expelled and end the day after he died."

"You're right, that is screwy," Jackson said, "but what does it mean?"

Xander rubbed his eyes and ran his hands through his hair. "I don't know yet. Some of my synapses went offline about 4 am and I don't think they're back yet."

The boys climbed out of the car and walked in opposite directions after Xander locked it.

"Good luck with that Lit test!" Jackson called.

"Oh, crap!" Xander said to himself.

When the lunch bell rang, students streamed out of all the classrooms to line up at the cafeteria window and the on-demand cafe room across from it.

"Jax!" Xander waved and shouted to Jackson from the front of the cafe line. "What do you want?"

"Turkey and chips!"

Xander picked up two sandwiches, a bag of Doritos, a bag of salt and pepper kettle chips, and two bottles of vitamin water then gave his student ID number to the woman at the cash register. He tossed items to Jackson while she rang him up.

"Let's go. We can eat on the way." He started to bite into his sandwich then said, "Maybe the whole meth thing isn't that implausible. Remember that principal in San Jose who got caught using drugs to get dates on a gay dating site?"

"Yeah . . . . ."

"So the whole teacher cooking meth isn't just on television. We know now that Missouri is some Midwest Methaven, right? And Josh's mom said Dr. Warner's been going there pretty regularly. There is more Sudafed in that locked cabinet than any one set of mucus membranes could possibly need, and she has access to all the chemicals required to process anything she wants," he paused to take a bite, chew and swallow. "And she has access to a buyer pool. She lives in San Francisco, I checked."

Jackson pulled up short. "Please tell me you did not just suggest that there is some kind of connection between meth and being gay."

"No, *buying* meth and being gay. Like the principal that got arrested."

"When you said your synapses hadn't kicked in, you weren't kidding." Jackson shook his head. "I'm going to tell Uncle John you said that."

Xander held up his hands. "Fine. If I picked a different statistically valid user pool would you feel better? Hookers in the Tenderloin? Or high school kids in Palo Alto? Or VCs on . . ." Xander's voice trailed off.

"What?"

"Cooking . . .," Xander said, frowning.

Jackson recognized the look and shook his head. "Never mind. Can you just try not to say anything that's going to get us expelled?"

Xander didn't answer as he continued toward the lab. Like all students, the boys were used to eating quickly while doing something else, so by the time they had walked back up to the science lab, they had each finished half a sandwich. Jackson stopped just short of the door to the lab and held out an arm to block Xander. He finished chewing a big bite and said, "Are we still all innocent and coy or are we going in Master Chief mode?"

Xander swallowed his own mouthful of sandwich. "I haven't spent enough bandwidth on Dr. Warner to justify full frontal assault. Low key."

Jackson nodded. "Yeah . . . I'll let her lead, anyway, since she asked for the meeting." He crammed half a sandwich into his backpack and opened his Doritos. He ate one, offered the bag to Xander, and took a deep breath. "Let's go."

The lab was empty.

Xander swung on Jackson with a scathing look. "Are you sure you had an appointment?"

"He is correct, Xander, though I didn't know you would be joining him." Dr. Warner stood up from behind the aquarium where, based on the eye dropper she held, she had been testing the water.

"Well, TJ was a . . . talkative guy," Xander said.

Jackson looked over at him, impressed he had come up with the implied spread of information as a form of protection. Or maybe he was just explaining his own presence, but it worked just the same. He faced Dr. Warner and said, "You asked to see me?" then smiled his most winning smile.

Dr. Warner walked over to where the boys stood, wiping her hands on her apron.   She closed the door and gestured toward the tables. "Have a seat. I don't think you boys know what you're actually dealing with."

Chapter 14

"What do you . . ." Xander started to speak, but Jackson pressed down on his toes under the table. Xander glared at him but didn't continue.

"Maybe you could explain it to us then," Jackson said.

Dr. Warner started to sit across from them, paused to take off her apron and fold it carefully. She placed it on the top of her desk and began to pace.

"TJ . . . thought . . . TJ found . . . TJ had some mistaken impressions. About me." She stopped and looked at the boys. "But we had already cleared those up before he . . ." She took a deep breath and let it out. "Whatever he told you, he would have changed the story." She looked at the floor. "If he had had time."

"Was TJ going to report you?" Xander asked.

Dr. Warner shook her head. "Not after I explained everything to him the last time I saw him. He understood the gray areas of moral compromise better than most adults I know."

Jackson and Xander exchanged a look, no longer sure they were all talking about the same thing and not sure where to go.

"My dad is dying." Dr. Warner bit her lower lip and her eyes welled up. A single tear spilled over and ran down her face.

Xander looked out the window, then fiddled with his nano watch band. Jackson lowered his eyes briefly, then studied Dr. Warner's response.

"We're sorry," he said when she seemed to be getting a grip on her emotions.

"Um, yeah," Xander added, "that must be . . . we're really sorry."

Dr. Warner almost smiled. "Thank you. It isn't a surprise, but . . . it goes on so much longer than you ever imagine possible . . . the pain . . . the travel . . . the never-ending bills. . . ."

Xander picked up where she left off. "So you started cooking meth to make ends meet."

Dr. Warner and Jackson looked at him with nearly identical expressions of shock.

"What?" Her tone was more perplexed than frightened.

"So much for low key," Jackson muttered.

"That's what TJ found out." Xander pressed.

"No . . . what? No, that's not. . . ." Dr. Warner was frowning and shaking her head as if to reset the conversation.

Jackson looked back and forth between the two of them, then said, "The acacia. From Texas?"

"Oh." Dr. Warner's face smoothed out. "Yes. Look. TJ found out I was ordering equipment and supplies for my own research using my school account. When he found out why I needed money, he said he'd keep my secret."

"He was going to blackmail you?" Jackson asked.

Dr. Warner shrugged and held up her hands. "I told you he understood moral ambiguity."

"No!" Xander insisted. "I don't believe TJ would believe that your dying father justified cooking meth!"

"What meth? There is no meth. I have a contract with a pharmaceutical company to find a way to extract the naturally occurring decongestant in specific strains of acacia plants. Imagine the market for a natural decongestant."

"What about all that Sudafed in your locked cabinet then?" Xander demanded.

Dr. Warner opened her mouth and closed it again. She walked over to the cabinet and unlocked it, swinging the doors open. "Come here."

The boys walked over to stand beside her.

"What Sudafed?"

"In the bottle labeled sucrose. Tell me those red tablets aren't really Sudafed" Xander said.

Dr. Warner and Jackson looked at the bottle, looked at Xander, looked at each other.

"Dude," Jackson said, "those tablets are *brown.*"

Xander flushed the color he thought the tablets were just as the lunch bell rang.

"You should get to class, " Dr. Warner said, "but I wanted you to know that I've already resigned. TJ's death was . . . a wake up call."

The Carter boys left Dr. Warner locking her cabinet and hurried out the door.

"Epic fail!" Jackson said.

"Hey, are you making fun of my disability?"

"Yeah, pretty much."

Woodhaven after school took on the split personality of casual socializers waiting to be picked up and focused students with sports practice or other obligations. Xander snagged a gatorade before the snack shack closed and leaned against one of the picnic tables watching Reza and Matthew play basketball while he jailbreaked a phone for a junior high kid. The day had been pretty much a total disaster, from falling asleep in Spanish to totally humiliating himself in front of both Dr. Warner and Jax. His friends motioned to him to join the game, but he waved them off. Xander used the school wifi to download the code he needed to release the iPhone from it's factory restrictions. He had done this so many times now, he could do it without thinking, the hacker version of touch-typing. His parents didn't know, but he got paid twenty bucks for every phone he "fixed" for one of his classmates. As he typed,

Xander's thoughts bounced around his fail day. He needed a better hack for Compton. And even if Dr. Warner had an explanation for everything, he felt like he'd missed something from the meeting.

"Hey, Xander."

He shifted his focus from internal to external. It took a minute to register who was talking to him even though he was looking right at her.

"Oh. Hey, Emily."

"You waiting for Jax?" She tilted her head toward the field where the soccer team was practicing. It made her hair fall across her face and she brushed it back behind her ear.

"Yeah. Do you need a ride?" He shook his head. "Never mind, I know you drove today. I think I'm sleep deprived."

"Maybe I should offer you a ride." She smiled

"I'm okay." He smiled back.

"Dude! Have you read your email?"

Ben skidded to a stop in front of Xander forming an isosceles triangle with Emily as the distant angle. After an awkward moment, he looked back and forth between Xander and Emily and said, "Oh, sorry. Am I interrupting?"

Emily shook her head. "No, I was just leaving. Thanks, again, for doing that article for me."

"No problem," Xander said.

They watched Emily walk away, then Ben said, "Did you read it?"

"My phone died and I left my powerbag at home." Xander shrugged. "What's up?"

"Get out your laptop. Compton wants to see you!"

Xander dug into his backpack and logged into his laptop. Typing furiously he said, "Did he say what he wants us for? Is it a follow-up to the presentation?"

"Not us, Xander, *you*! Compton wants a meeting with just you. As soon as possible." Ben shifted his weight from one foot to the other. "What should we do?"

Xander read the terse email over and over, hoping for some subtext, but he couldn't get anything. "So much for buying more time. I need to go back there." He ran his hands through his hair and scanned the kids left on campus. "I can't talk to him without more data." He couldn't take his car back to Digital Capital, but if someone gave him a ride, maybe he could get access to Compton's computer through the spider. He briefly considered, then rejected Emily just as Dr. Warner walked past the lockers on her way to the parking lot.

"If Jax comes off the field, tell him I'll be back," Xander said to Ben as he crammed his laptop into his backpack and ran after the science teacher.

"Dr. Warner!" He caught up to her and matched his pace to hers. "I have a really big favor to ask."

She stopped and turned to face him, searching his eyes with a piercing look that made him take a step back. "I didn't take you for the blackmail sort."

His eyes opened wide. "No, no, it's not like that!" Xander glanced toward the field then plunged ahead. "I just . . . need a ride to Sandhill Road and back. Right now."

Dr. Warner frowned and tilted her head. "Is there a problem with your car?"

"No. I mean yes, there is a . . . problem . . . with my car. Please?" He slung his backpack over his shoulder and looked at the ground. "I totally understand if you're busy. I didn't mean to make it sound like a threat."

She shook her head. "Well . . . considering you didn't go immediately to the office to report me, I think I can take you where you need to go.."

"Thank you, Dr. Warner!"

Xander pulled his laptop out of his bag as soon as he got into Dr. Warner's Prius and started flipping through screens. There were no words spoken on the drive except Xander's instructions to Digital Capital, but it was not an uncomfortable silence.

When they made the turn into the parking lot, Xander said, "Drive straight back and pull into any space." He typed furiously, then looked up. "Please."

Dr. Warner smiled to herself and parked the car. After Xander had typed for a few minutes without saying anything, she asked, "Are you going in?"

He stopped typing, closed the laptop, and turned to Dr. Warner. "No. Let's go." He shoved the laptop back into the backpack with a big sigh. "The spider's dead."

Chapter 15

"I'm not sure how to ask this . . . ," Dr. Warner began as she pulled out of the lot, "but . . . spider? Is that a euphemism? Why were we here?"

Xander ran both hands back and forth through his hair so hard it seemed he was trying to stimulate brain cells instead of just follicles.

"I . . . uh . . . there was a contest . . .," he blew out his breath. "It's complicated."

They rode in silence for several minutes. Finally Xander said, "I don't think TJ killed himself." He turned toward Dr. Warner. "I think someone inside that building did."

Dr. Warner's face was skeptical, then her eyes opened wide. "You thought I did it."

"Well, you were . . . a possibility."

She nodded. "Based on what you thought was going on, that would be a reasonable conclusion. If he didn't kill himself."

Gratified by her acknowledgement, Xander added, "Good thing you didn't meet him at the Coffee House the night he died."

"How did you know?"

Dr. Warner's voice had changed completely, and for one second Xander wished Jax had come with them.

"What?"

"How did you know I met him at Stanford?"

"You met him at Stanford the night before he died?"

The silence that filled the car this time was not comfortable. Xander slowly moved his hand to the door armrest and slid his foot through the backpack straps. if he needed to exit the car suddenly, he was prepared.

Dr. Warner's grip on the wheel left her knuckles white. Xander watched her out of the corner of his eye, but she never glanced over at him. As they approached the school, Xander suddenly sat straight up in the seat.

"Wait! Pull over!"

Dr. Warner looked over at him in surprise and did what he asked.

"What time did you meet TJ?"

"Eight o'clock. Well, a bit after. I was running late." She frowned. "Why?"

Xander dug out his laptop, entered his password, and started typing. He swung it around to show her the screen filled with the same photos he had shown to Nicholas.

"Did you see any of these men in the COHO that night?"

The science teacher first scanned the group then scrutinized each photo, shaking her head to herself.

"I don't really remember anything about the other people there. But this guy," she tapped the screen, "looks like the guy who almost ran me down in the parking lot because he was on his phone."

Xander angled the lap top for a better view. She'd picked Compton.

"Yes! Dr. Warner, this is so great!"

Xander laid out his theory of TJ's murder from the planted vodka in the locker to the nike plus tracker to the app pitch at Digital Capital.

"So I still don't know what he had against TJ, but I know he's involved," he finished. "And now I have you putting him at the COHO."

" If you really think this man had something to do with TJ's death, you need to go to the police." Dr. Warner searched Xander's face. "You know I can't be involved in this, don't you? If I say I was meeting TJ, I'll have to explain why. I can't . . . I can't let my father down now."

"But what am I supposed to say to the police if you don't . . .," Xander had nothing to add, nowhere to go with his objection. He slumped in the seat.

"I'm sorry." Dr. Warner pulled back onto the street.

"I get it."

They didn't speak again until Dr. Warner pulled into the circular drive to drop him off in the Woodhaven parking lot.

Xander climbed out, grabbed his backpack, and leaned into the car. "Thanks for the ride."

"I really am . . ."

Xander closed the door.

Mona Carter was walking out just as the boys pulled into the driveway.

"Perfect timing!" She smiled. "It's book club night. I left tuna salad and avocado in the refrigerator, and if you don't feel like that, there's ham and cheese for sandwiches. Your dad will be home later."

"Thanks, Mom," Jackson said.

"Yeah, thanks. Is there fruit?" Xander asked.

"If not," Mona said, "pick some oranges. Have a great evening!" She waved to the boys as she drove away.

"Halo when you're done with homework?" Jackson asked.

Xander dropped his backpack and walked toward the kitchen.

"Really? Wow!"

"What?" Xander turned around.

"I just asked if you wanted to play Halo."

"Yeah, but I don't think that's going to happen. I put Compton off until tomorrow, but I'm supposed to be at Capital Digital at eight."

Jackson shrugged. "So?"

Xander pulled the tuna and avocado out of the refrigerator and heaped some on a plate. He added a couple slices of cheese and a pickle. "So I need an angle on this guy. With the spider gone, I've got to go through every bit of data I got from the download."

"What about Dr. Warner?"

Xander shook his head as he poured a glass of milk. "She isn't going to help. She didn't actually see him with TJ, anyway." He shoved a box of rosemary crackers under his arm and picked up his dinner. "I'll be in my room."

Hours later, after Dave Carter had come home and checked in, after Mona Carter had come home and said good night, Xander sent a text to Jackson and waited. He checked to see if Jackson was in the middle of a game, but he was offline. Xander sighed and dialed Jackson's number, knowing he was taking a risk that their dad would hear it. Through the wall he could hear the strains of the

Doctor Who theme song, his personal ring tone on Jackson's phone.

"What . . . are you crazy or just a jerk? I'm trying to sleep!"

"Google hang out right now," Xander whispered. "Ben's

already there."

Xander listened intently for the sounds of adult feet in the

hallway, but all was quiet. "Okay, keep your voices down," he said

as join as Jackson joined.

"This better be good." Jackson yawned.

"I have a theory . . ."

"Oh, god. You woke me up for this?" Jackson asked.

" . . . about Compton," Xander continued, ignoring Jackson.

"His deleted email from around the time TJ was killed included a lot

of mail to the CEO of SpitTake, a company that had applied for

funding from Digital Capital."

"SpitTake?" Jackson's voice was withering.

"What did they say?" Ben asked.

"That's just it. Nothing. They were all blank."

Ben looked perplexed. "Then why delete them?"

"Exactly!" Xander tried to stifle his exuberance and lowered his voice again. "I think the blank mails were a signal to call or meet."

"Is your point even remotely close to this time zone?"

"Relax, Jax! You have to hear it all to see if it makes sense."

"Fine."

"Compton is also on the board of StemPunk, a company that uses adult T-cells and cord blood stem cells for treating Parkinson's, Alzheimer's, and a bunch of other things."

"Cord blood?" Ben asked.

"Yeah. Umbilical cord."

"Eww, gross!"

Xander waved off the aside. "Here's where the speculation comes in. SpitTake has developed a home saliva testing kit that will allow you to test for five genetic markers for two hundred dollars."

"So they're like 23andMe," Ben said.

"No. They aren't running your genome, that's why it costs so much less. They look at the five things you choose from their list."

"And if testing this cheap and easy were widely available," Jackson started.

"The StemPunk stock would skyrocket," Xander finished. "Not to mention if there's a SpitTake IPO."

"This is vaguely plausible, but where does TJ come in?" Jackson asked.

"So we think TJ must have met Compton the night of his daughter's volleyball game, right?"

"Maybe," Jackson said.

"Suppose TJ heard Compton on one of his secret phone calls? Maybe he was pacing the back hall away from the gym or standing near the back parking lot and TJ ran into him on his way to his locker."

Ben nodded. "That could happen."

Jackson heaved a big sigh. "That's a reach. Do we even know TJ was there? Why would he go to his locker? Why would Compton care if some kid saw him?"

Xander held up his hand. "The Student Council goes to every game unless they have a major conflict. No idea about the locker, but Compton knew where to deliver the lunch, and I think TJ must have not just run into him, but overheard enough to make Compton nervous."

The three sat looking at each other on the screen without speaking.

"You think it was some kind of insider trading thing?" Jackson finally asked.

"Whatever it was," Xander said, "I think Compton was willing to kill TJ to make sure no one else found out."

Chapter 16

"Xander, time to get up." Mona leaned into the room and spoke softly. "Xander," she raised her voice, "it's after seven."

"Mom!" he mumbled from under the covers, "I'm not five!"

"Yeah," Mona said, "you're also not up. Do you want some orange juice?"

"No."

As Mona walked away she heard "Thanks, Mom . . ." and wondered if she would need to make a return trip. She heard Jackson in the bathroom and paused outside the door.

"Sweetie? Would you check to make sure Xander's up when you come out?"

"Okay, Mom."

Mona walked to the kitchen, poured herself a cup of coffee, and continued out to her studio. As she opened the door she paused, frowning and looking toward the boys' rooms. Jackson's willingness to check on Xander without complaint didn't seem quite right, but she shook it off and went to work.

"Get up already, loner!" Jackson smacked the bottom of Xander's foot.

Xander groaned and shifted position, posed vaguely like the outline of an accident victim. "Okay. Okay." He swung his feet over the edge of the bed and sat up without opening his eyes. "I'm up." He made a dismissive gesture with his fingers. "You can go now."

The morning shifted into running-late overdrive as the textbook, backpack, clothes, milk, muffin, toothpaste, run to the car school routine became a frenzy. The Carter boys didn't speak at all until they were almost to school.

"So are we clear on tonight?" Xander said as they hit the winding stretch of road just before the Woodhaven drive. He looked over at Jackson then punched him in the arm.

"What the . . .?" Jackson yanked out his left earbud.

"I said, 'Are we clear on tonight?'."

Jackson glared at his brother. "Yeah. I wait in the car, you call me and leave your phone on so I can listen, just as a precaution, because there will probably still be other people in the building." He recited it as if quoting a dull text he'd been forced to memorize. "I still think this is a bad idea. For the record."

"For the record, he threatened to disqualify us if I didn't show tonight."

Jackson threw up his hands. "What do you care? The whole app pitch was just to get to Compton."

"Exactly. If we get booted now, we lose our best chance of getting to the truth."

Jackson shrugged. "You could always kidnap his daughter." When Xander didn't say anything, he looked at him sharply. Xander was lost in thought as if he might be considering the possibility. "Just . . . stop." Jackson held up a hand. "We'll stick with the plan we've got." He shook his head. "You know, sometimes you scare me."

Xander gave his website update to the Journalism lunch meeting then asked to be excused early. He sat searching and typing through the rest of the break, barely touching his sandwich. He wanted to go in to the meeting with Compton with as much information about SpitTake and StemPunk as possible. Knowledge was more than power, as far as Xander was concerned, it was a shield.

"You going to eat that?" Reza asked.

"Go 'head." Xander slid the sandwich toward him without looking away from the screen.

"Dude!" Reza said, "It's a BLT!"

"So?" Ben asked.

"Um . . . I don't eat pork?"

"Oh, man! Bacon counts? Shouldn't that be exempt? I mean, even vegans should get to eat bacon." Ben shook his head. "That just seems wrong that people can't eat bacon."

Matthew laughed with a mouthful of vitamin water and started choking but managed not to have it come out his nose.

"No points," Reza said.

Xander reached over, pulled the bacon out of the sandwich and folded it into his mouth. He wiped his fingers on his pants and went back to typing. "Now it's just an LT."

"Trolled!" Ben said to Reza.

"Hard!" Matthew added.

Reza shrugged and picked up the sandwich. "I can live with that."

As people started packing up, Ben turned to Xander. "Sorry I have to work tonight."

Xander shut down his laptop. "It's okay, man. I'll have Jax in the parking lot. We ought to get something tonight, one way or another, and I don't think it will be too late. We'll stop by Pizza My Mind on the way home to fill you in."

"Sounds good."

Ben's next class was at the far end of campus, so he left Xander packing up.

"Are you ever not totally surrounded by people?"

Xander looked up to find Emily standing beside him. He shouldered his backpack.

"I . . . don't know."

Emily laughed and shook her head. "No, you probably don't."

"I'm walking this way." Xander gestured in the general direction of his Spanish class.

"Me, too."

They walked together for a few moments before Emily said, "I was thinking about putting together a suicide prevention support group for local high school kids. I've been meeting with Ms Teeter . . . I thought maybe you would help me with the website?"

"Suicide?" Xander asked, maybe too harshly, based on Emily's expression. "I mean . . . ," of course she still thought TJ had committed suicide. " . . . no problem. I'd be glad to."

"Could you come over tonight?"

They stopped outside the Spanish classroom. Xander looked at Emily, trying to decide how much to tell her. "I have something else tonight," he said, "but I'm going to . . . I'm working on something for TJ."

Emily had a strange sort of teary-eyed smile as she put her hand on his arm. "Really? Can I see it?"

The bell rang. "You'd better hurry," he said, lifting his chin. He called after her as she jogged away, "When I'm finished with this, you will definitely know."

"Hey, Jax!" Josh's twin sister and her friends clustered around the two boys as they walked past the bench where the freshmen congregated for pick up after school.

"Hey, Emma," Jackson responded. Josh elbowed him, but Jackson ignored it. "Priya, new hair? Looks good."

Priya blushed and lowered her eyes. "Yeah, thanks for noticing."

"What about me? Notice anything new?" Siobhan twirled in place.

"No, dude. Same old same old," Jackson said. He ducked as she tried to slap the back of his head.

"I am not a dude!"

"Yeah, Shivvy, that's pretty obvious," Jackson said. "Are you sure that sweater isn't a dress code violation?"

She smiled. "No visible cleavage."

Jackson shook his head and smiled. "Not for lack of trying."

"Fail!" Josh rolled his eyes. "There's mom." He paused as the girls climbed into the car. "Planetary Annihilation later?"

Jackson shook his head, "No . . . I'll be . . . wait, yeah. I've got a block of dead time tonight where I'll just be sitting around. I'll log in around eight."

Jackson walked over to Xander's car and leaned against it. He dropped his backpack to the ground and thumbed the surface of his phone with a speed that made it look like he had a medical condition.

"Jax?"

Jackson started, fumbled his phone but secured it before it hit the ground. Nicholas had materialized into his lack of attention as if by magic.

"Dude! Do not sneak up on me like that."

"Sorry," Nicholas said. "But I thought you should know."

Jackson sighed. "Know what, Nicholas?"

"I saw TJ's dad again today."

"We went over this, remember? TJ didn't have a dad?"

"No, I remember. I mean that guy who brought the lunch. The one in the pictures. He was here."

Jackson stopped typing and became very still. "That man was on campus today?"

Nicholas nodded.

"Where?" Jackson asked.

"He was in the office."

The boys stood in silence, then Nicholas said, "I have to go."

"Yeah, of course," Jackson focused back on Nicholas. "Thanks."

Xander walked up as Nicholas was leaving. He unlocked the car and dumped his backpack.

"What are you waiting for, loner? Get in the car. Let's go!"

Jackson put his backpack in the car but didn't get in. "Did you see Nicholas?"

"What? When? No." Xander got behind the wheel and started the car.

"He saw Parker Compton on campus today. In the office, but still . . ."

Xander looked at Jackson and cut the engine. "Let's go check our lockers before we leave, just in case."

Chapter 17

"I thought you were going to be home for dinner."

"Sorry, Mom. I totally forgot."

Jackson looked from his brother to his mom and back again. Xander was totally engrossed in the details of Compton's business life, so much so that he was about to get grounded and miss the meeting.

"We *are* going to be home, Mom." Jackson smiled and ignored the glare he could feel singeing the right side of his face. "We just have stuff after dinner and were hoping to eat early." He turned to Xander and raised his eyebrows. "That's all, right?

"Oh . . . right. Isn't that what I said?" Xander shrugged and smiled.

Mona shook her head. "And what's up tonight?"

Xander was ready for this one. "Emily asked me to help her set up a suicide prevention website." It wasn't a lie. It just wasn't what he was was doing tonight.

Mona's face shifted through several emotions before she squeezed Xander's arm and smiled. "Emily's a nice girl. It's good of you to help." She turned to Jackson. "You're going, too?"

"No . . ." Jackson hadn't heard Xander's backstory plan, so he had to improvise. "I'm going to do some gaming with Josh. But Xander's driving." It wasn't a lie, because he would be gaming with Josh, just not at his house.

"Okay. I can move up dinner by half an hour. I'll call Dad."

The boys walked toward their rooms as Mona went to the kitchen.

"Suicide prevention?" Jackson said under his breath.

"Seriously. She asked. I told her not tonight."

Jackson punched his brother in the arm. "Could you at least pretend to understand that I am not automatically copied on all your thoughts telepathically? At least until the iChip comes out."

Xander looked wistful for a moment at the mention of the iChip, then shook his head and punched Jackson back. "You do some more checking on StemPunk and SpitTake while I recheck the deleted emails and see if I can get into his confidential files."

"I'm doing my homework first."

"Lone!" Xander snorted in disgust and walked into his room, starting his computer and then his laptop. He was about to open the deleted messages folder when he paused and instead sorted All Mail by date. Maybe what he needed wasn't in the things Compton tried to bury, maybe it was right out in the open. Xander scrolled to the day TJ died and started working backward.

"So what's going on in school boys?" Dave Carter asked between bites of salad.

"Well . . .," Xander began, "they're looking at starting school two weeks earlier next year so finals will be before Christmas and the editor of *The Word* is writing an editorial advocating that Elliot be able to keep his mohawk despite the dress code."

"We have to go back to school in the middle of August? What are they thinking?" Jackson practically shouted.

Mona finished chewing a bite and said, "Nice to have the finals before vacation, though, right?"

Dave lifted one corner of his mouth. "Nice to hear the editor is using his platform to a good end. Today mohawks, tomorrow shorts."

"I know, right?" Jackson said. "I haven't worn long pants to school in, like, three years."

Xander gave him a withering look. "I'm pretty sure that it's supposed to be funny."

"The editorial or Dad?"

"Both."

Mona laughed.

"Har. Har," Dave said. "And what about your app pitch at Digital Capital? When do you hear something?"

The boys both shoveled in a spoonful of chili and took a bite of cornbread as if on a synchronized eating team, holding up a finger while they chewed. They did not exchange a look, each dragging out the bite, hoping the other would speak first. Xander lost.

"Today was the last round of pitch sessions," he said. "The winners will be posted tomorrow at midnight."

"What are your chances?"

Xander shot a glance to Jackson as he considered the question. Chances of getting anything out of Compton tonight? Chances of getting justice for TJ? Chances of being chosen one of the three winning apps on a pitch he practically made up on the spot?

"Not very good." He shrugged. "But it was worth it."

Dave looked down at his plate. "What did you think of Compton?"

Xander felt Jackson's foot on his and resisted the urge to punch him in the arm.

"Nice suit. Kind of a jerk. But the other two were pretty much the same."

Dave nodded. "Well, I hope it goes well, but if he makes you any kind of offer, I want to see it before you sign anything."

"Still a minor, Dad. Can't sign contracts. I'm not an idiot."

"That's debatable," Jackson said.

"Boys," Mona intervened. She gave Xander an expectant look. "Xander?"

"Sorry Dad."

"I know you're not an idiot, I just doubt that you've dealt with anyone quite like Compton."

"Do you know him?" Xander asked.

Dave shook his head. "No. But I know his reputation. He skirts the legal boundaries on deals and is not just ruthless in business, he's vindictive. I've seen what happened to people who got in his way."

Both boys looked up, then tried not to look too interested.

"What happened?" Jackson asked.

"Bankruptcy, divorce, even suicide." Dave looked at Xander hard. "He isn't a businessman, he's a predator. Don't be fooled by the suit."

"Are you ready?" Xander dialed Jackson's number then slipped his own phone into his shirt pocket and zipped his hoodie halfway up to keep it covered. "I'll do a sound check when I get to the door. If you can't hear me when I get inside, hang up and call me back."

"Won't Compton be suspicious?"

"Nah. I'll just make it look like I'm silencing my phone."

"What if you don't answer?"

"Well . . . ," Xander looked at Jackson, "then you'd better figure out what's going on."

Jackson sighed. "Great."

"I'm sure it will be fine," Xander said. "I've got a back up plan." He climbed out of the car, slammed the door and started across the parking lot. "I'm at the door."

"I can see that."

"That was a sound check, loner."

Xander walked through the empty lobby and down the hallway toward the only office with its light on. He paused in the doorway and Parker Compton looked up from his computer.

"Mr. Carter, I'm so pleased you were able to meet." He gestured to a chair in front of the desk as he rose. "Have a seat."

Xander swallowed and cleared his throat. "Thanks. I'm sorry Ben couldn't be here. Did you need something more on Pigs for Peace?"

Compton walked out from behind the desk and leaned against it, inches from Xander, so close their feet almost touched. Xander shifted in the chair but maintained eye contact. The corner's of Compton's mouth were lifted as if he were smiling, but the look in his eyes was something Xander had never seen.

"I think you know you're not here to talk about your little app," Compton said. "We're here to give you a chance to tell me why I shouldn't turn you over to the police."

He held up the spider and dangled it in front of Xander's face like a hypnotist. Xander watched the spider swing back and forth, so focused on running through his options that it took him a moment to realize that in his other hand Compton was holding plastic cable tie handcuffs.

Chapter 18

Jackson listened with half an ear to the conversation Xander was having with Compton as he moved his avatar through a rocky landscape on the iPad screen. It had started with, "I believe this is yours." followed by a soft smacking sound. Jackson figured it was the Nano. He had turned off the sound on the iPad, so he and Josh were exchanging text comments only. Playing with a headset was much easier, but he was on radio silence since his phone line was open. When Jackson heard Xander say, "Go ahead, call the police." it took a second to sink in. Was it just a statement to Compton or a request for him? Jackson stopped playing and listened.

"I think they'll be more interested in you than in me."

"I have no idea what you're talking about. You were obviously trying to game the contest or worse. Maybe you're a freelance hacker selling insider information."

Jackson bet Xander wished he had thought of that. Compton's voice continued.

"I have nothing to hide."

"That's because it hasn't happened yet."

What? Jackson mouthed. Where the heck was Xander going?

"I read the draft of the Board Report. And all those partnership agreement memos. You're about to announce that you're moving on, but your partners are throwing you out."

"Very clever. But nothing the police would care about."

Compton's voice sounded different. Jackson turned the volume on his phone all the way up.

"Maybe not. Maybe it isn't even fraud to build up StemPunk and SpitTake just to tank them and screw your partners . . . but I'm pretty sure they care about murder."

Compton barked a horrible sort of laugh that made the hair stand up on the back of Jackson's neck.

"Well, aren't you just the little Sherlock. You've still got nothing."

"You weren't the only one TJ was blackmailing. Someone saw you at the Coffee House."

The car was filled with sounds of scraping and grunting, shouting and crashing, then the call was disconnected. Jackson stared at his phone as if it were possessed. He dialed Xander's number then hung up before it connected. He opened the car door, closed it again.

"WWXD. . . WWXD . . .," he muttered to himself and he drummed his hands nervously on the passenger seat.

He looked down at the game. Josh's avatar wasn't moving, but he hadn't logged out. He started to call, then decided he should leave the phone line open. Jackson started typing.

911! 911! Send police to Digital Capital. NOW!

Jackson bolted from the car and started running toward the building. He stopped abruptly, ran back to the car, popped the trunk and grabbed the tire iron before tearing full speed to the front door and throwing it open. He paused in the lobby, then lifted the tire iron like a baseball bat and advanced down the hallway toward

Compton's office. He wished he had body armor. Or a sniper rifle. Or a sticky detonator. Or a warthog. Or back up.

There was a thumping from inside the office, something irregular but rhythmic like moving furniture. Jackson pressed his back up against the wall. Blowing through the door probably made too much noise. On the other hand, he had no idea what was going on. He took a deep breath then launched himself around the door jam and into the room with the tire iron held up ready to strike.

Xander was on the floor with his hands and feet bound with plastic and duct tape over his mouth. A chair was overturned beside him and he was trying to say something. Jackson dropped to the floor and tore off the duct tape as Xander's eyes got wide.

"Ow! You moron!"

Compton stepped out from behind the door and kicked the tire iron out of reach.

"How could you not check behind the door? N00b!"

"Hey, in real life I don't have a map or infrared goggles."

"And I thought girls were a pain in the ass." Compton picked up the tire iron and gestured with it. "Shut up, both of you.

You, grab that duct tape and wrap your ankles. I didn't bring plastic cuffs enough for surprise guests."

When Jackson finished, Compton wrapped his wrists, too, then picked the chair up and sat in it facing the boys with the tire iron across his knees. He squinted and drummed his fingers on the metal rod.

"Well . . . what now?"

"You let us go?" Jackson asked hopefully.

Compton looked disgusted. "That was a rhetorical question. I need to stash you someplace until my flight leaves tomorrow. My last client meetings in London and Brussels seemed like the perfect time to start a long vacation." He smiled at Xander. "And watch the firm collapse from a distance. The flight from prosecution is just icing."

"That won't work," Xander said quietly.

"Really? I can stick you in one of several unused guest houses in Atherton and you can wait for the gardner to find you. If you're lucky it won't be more than a day or two."

"I set a time-delay auto-send on my home computer before I left. If I don't turn it off by eleven, all the data I have, including the name of the witness, go to the police. You won't make that flight."

"Oh, please!" Compton rolled his eyes.

"Dude!" Jackson said. "Think about it. The spider? He would so do that. Seriously."

"I am *not* a dude."

Jackson snickered involuntarily and Compton slammed the tire iron down on the desk, splintering the edge of the polished wood.

"Maybe I should just beat you both to a bloody pulp and leave you here then!"

His face was blotchy and his eyes bulged. Both boys grew instantly still.

Compton took a deep breath and adjusted his suit jacket. He stood abruptly, blew out his breath and walked around the desk. He didn't bother sitting down, just started typing. "I can get a new ticket right now."

"No. You can't."

Jackson looked at Xander. The cut over his left eye was bleeding and his lower lip was swollen. Beneath the red smears he was noticeably pale.

Compton typed faster and louder, growing more frustrated as they watched. Finally he slammed the laptop closed.

"What did you do?" Compton's voice was perfectly calm and barely audible, somehow even scarier than the yelling.

"Too many incorrect password login attempts. On all the accounts I could find. The fraud alert calls . . . might not have gone through."

Jackson looked from Compton to Xander and back again. He couldn't be sure when or if Josh would get his message, but they definitely needed more time.

"But we could get you a new ticket. Right now."

Compton made a face. "Oh, really? What with, your trust fund?"

Jackson looked at Xander. "No. Paypal."

Xander nodded and smiled a grim smile.

Jackson turned to Compton and summoned all the sincerity he could find. "You don't have to kill us. We can help you get away."

"Are you trying to make a deal?"

Jackson shrugged. "Do you blame me?"

Compton looked at him long and hard, but Jackson didn't look away, though he did swallow hard.

Xander cleared his throat. "Undo my hands and give back my phone and I can get you on the first flight to anywhere."

"On, no!" Compton pointed the tire iron at him. "No phone for you. Use my computer." He gestured with the iron. "Let's see what you can do, and then I'll decide."

Compton cut the plastic tie around his ankles and Xander struggled to his feet then held his hands out to have the cuff cut off. Compton stepped back to let him pass.

"I'm sure you can type well enough."

Jackson watched Compton as Xander typed. The man's face was flushed and he was sweating, but he had let the tire iron drop to his side. He wiped his forehead and rubbed his temples. He looked more sick than violent. More panicked than evil. But he still had them tied up. Jackson decided to to try a new version of the story.

"If you didn't mean to kill TJ, you don't even have to run. He was blackmailing you, right? Maybe it was self-defense. Or an accident."

"What?" Parker Compton turned to Jackson with a funny expression. "How did you know?"

Xander looked up from the computer briefly, then went back to typing.

"I was just trying to scare him . . .," he looked almost wistful for an instant, then his face hardened. "It doesn't matter." He tightened his grip on the iron and turned to Xander. "Well?"

"I can get you on a midnight flight to Hong Kong out of SFO. Plenty of time for us to get home and stop the file transfer."

Compton looked at the PayPal screen Xander had open and nodded. "Buy it," he said, and when Xander had completed the transaction he added, "But you're not going home."

Chapter 19

"You're not going anywhere."

Compton ran his hands through his hair vigorously enough to pass for a scalp massage, then took a deep breath and smoothed his hair into place. Xander looked across the desk to where Jackson was sitting on the floor. Jackson cleared his throat.

"You're leaving us here for the security guard to find?"

Compton snorted as he adjusted his collar and shirt cuffs. "Nice try, kid. You're coming to the airport with me. The police won't do anything tonight based on some random email. They probably won't even open it until morning."

"Isn't that a big risk?" Xander asked.

"I've taken bigger." Compton shrugged. He gestured for Xander to sit, then cut the duct tape to free Jackson's feet. He stood well back and gestured toward the door, jingling Xander's car keys. "Let's go. And don't even think of running."

"Can I go to the bathroom first?" Jackson asked.

"You can wait," Compton said.

"I don't think so."

"Please don't let him pee in my car," Xander said. He glared at Jackson.

A funny little half smile appeared and vanished, and Compton nodded to himself. "Fine."

They walked to the Men's room and Compton stood in the doorway, holding the door open. "Hurry." He turned to Xander. "You need to go, too?"

"I'm okay."

"Then sit with your back against the wall."

Compton pulled out his phone and started texting furiously, impeded slightly by the tire iron in one hand. He looked rapidly back and forth between the screen and Xander, making sure he wasn't trying to get up. He pocketed his phone just as the urinal flushed, and they all walked out of the building in single file, Xander in the lead and Compton bringing up the rear.

"Turn left. I need to get my bag."

Compton directed them to a black Mercedes so new it didn't even have plates yet.

"You have a V12?" Xander said. "Can we take your car?"

Compton took a duffle from the trunk and waved the boys away, ignoring Xander's request. "Where to?"

As they approached his car with Jackson in the lead, Xander spotted the open trunk.

"You left the trunk open? Did you even bother to lock it?"

"I was in kind of a hurry, remember?"

Compton shoved Xander from behind with the tire iron so he stumbled into Jackson and then the car. "Don't make me go back for the duct tape."

Xander started around to the driver's side.

"Unh-uh. As long as the trunk's open, your little brother can ride there."

"No way!" Jackson yelled. "That's his gym bag in there! I don't think he washes anything ever. Make him get in the trunk."

"I'm not getting in the trunk," Xander said, indignantly. "It's not like you have a gun!"

Compton slammed the tire iron against the trunk lid, leaving a big dent. Both boys flinched.

"Are you sure?" The boys were silent. Compton slammed the lid closed and gestured toward the passenger door. Xander opened it, and Jackson's iPad, still balanced between the seats, slid to the floor.

"Fold the seat down."

When Xander had complied, Compton nudged Jackson with the tire iron and continued directing Xander.

"When he gets in, latch the seat belt through his hands."

Jackson maneuvered into the back, catching his foot between the seat and the door and falling sideways as he yanked it free. Compton monitored the process of Xander buckling Jackson in then stepped back.

"Now you."

Xander picked the iPad up off the floor and wedged it beside the seat before performing his own elaborate wrestling match with the seatbelt as Compton watched.

"Don't do anything stupid," Compton said as he adjusted the mirrors and started the car.

"Too late," Jackson muttered under his breath.

"What's that?"

"Nothing."

Compton pulled up to the stop sign at the parking lot exit and stalled out. "What kind of idiot doesn't drive an automatic? I'd have an autonomous vehicle if Google would sell me one."

He turned right, away from the freeway.

"Aren't we going the wrong way?" Xander asked.

"I have something to do before the airport."

They traveled in silence but for the occasional grunts of irritation when Compton downshifted as he navigated to Junipero Serra. Jackson watched Compton's profile as the street lights flashed past. There was something wrong with his face, like parts of it didn't match. He was almost smiling, well, more like smirking, really, but when his eyes met Jackson's for a second in the rearview mirror, they were cold and empty. It reminded Jackson of the shark in the big tank at the Monterey Aquarium.

Junipero Serra became Foothill Expressway, but when Compton turned onto Arastradero, the route looked a little too familiar. Jackson could hear Xander's fingers drumming, meaning he was deep into some problem, hopefully their current one. Jackson wouldn't bet on it, though. He cleared his throat.

"Where do you live?"

Compton flicked his eyes up to the rearview mirror and back to the road without answering.

The first few bars of the Ode to Joy suddenly filled the car. Compton's eyes narrowed as he turned to Xander. "Who is it?"

Xander shrugged. "Just Mom."

They crossed El Camino, and Arastradero became Charleston.

"Xander?" Jackson's voice was higher than normal, but nothing he could do about it.

The car swerved to the right a block before the same train crossing where TJ died. TJ and almost a dozen other people over the years. Compton slid out of the car, pulled his bag out and dropped it on the curb beside a bush. He climbed back behind the wheel and made a U-turn, idling at the intersection while he looked at his phone.

"Um . . . should we get out here?" Jackson asked.

Compton snorted. Suddenly he jammed the phone in his pocket and accelerated around the corner, stopping the car on the northbound tracks. He turned off the car, jumped out and threw the keys down the tracks, then reached in and cut the zip tie on Xander's wrists and the duct tape on Jackson's. He held the tire iron up in one hand to make sure they didn't leave the car.

"Maybe you'll get lucky and one of those rent-a-cops will turn up before your terrible accident happens." He raised his head and squinted south toward a tiny point of light. "I don't think so, though." Compton heaved a dramatic sigh. "Teenage boys take so many risks . . . like racing trains."

"Wait!" Jackson said as he struggled with his duct tape. "You don't have to . . . you can't just kill people!"

"Really?" Compton said. "How many men have you knifed and shot and blown up in your video game career?"

"Those aren't real people," Jackson said.

Compton shook his head slowly, as if explaining something to a child. "Neither are you." He started to close the door, then leaned back in and swung the tire iron at Jackson's head. The roof caught most of the blow, but Jackson slumped sideways. Compton grinned and saluted. "Gotta run. My driver is waiting."

He knocked on Xander's window. "Thanks for the ticket. I'm pretty sure the concierge in the club lounge will be able to move mine to an earlier flight, but yours provides a nice distraction."

And then he was gone, running back toward where he'd stashed his bag.

"Let's go!" Xander shouted. He already had his seat belt unlatched and was popping the door. He fell out onto the tracks, Jackson's iPad tumbling after him.

Jackson hadn't lost consciousness, but his vision was blurry. The seatbelt was undone, but every time he tried to push the seat forward, the lever slipped out of his hands. He finally got it just as Xander was reaching for it and half dived half fell out of the car.

"I was able to get a check-in at Gunn on your iPad, but I don't think the Walgreens one went through." Xander yelled. "I just hope Ben sees it."

He looked down at Jackson floundering on the ground. The light was much bigger now, and they could hear the train.

"Stop fooling around!" Xander yelled.

"I'm stuck!" Jackson was kicking to free his legs, but his left foot got twisted between the seat and the door frame, just like always.

The train blasted its horn as the headlamp lit up the car.

Jackson looked up at Xander and whacked at his leg with one hand as he struggled with the seat. "Go! You have to get out of the way!"

"No!" Xander grabbed Jackson's hands and pulled, leaning back away from the tracks with his full weight and jerking hard with each word. "I. Am. Not. Leaving. YOU!"

The train brakes screamed as the engine plowed into the car . . . and the night filled with sounds of grinding metal and breaking glass.

Chapter 20

"Mom?"

Jackson could smell his mother's perfume. He opened his eyes and tried to focus. His eyelids were gummy, and he had to blink hard several times to clear his vision. The light was too bright, forcing him to squint until his eyes adjusted.

"I'm right here, sweetie."

Mona brushed a curl off his forehead and shielded his eyes with her hand. Jackson opened his eyes wider and could see her smile, but she was pale and her eyes were red.

"And here would be . . . . where exactly?"

Mona's laughed sounded like stereo, and Jackson turned away from her to locate the other voice. It was Xander standing on the other side of the bed.

"You're in the hospital, loner! Took you long enough to wake up." Sounded like the usual Xander, but his eyes had dark circles under them. He was also covered with scratches.

Jackson frowned and tried to think about time. The last thing he remembered was the car. And the train. He looked down the bed and saw the cast on his leg. An image of Xander yanking on his arms came back to him.

"Did you break my leg?"

"Fail! I'm pretty sure I saved your life. A little gratitude might be in order."

Jackson rubbed his forehead. He was foggy and achey and his tongue felt twice its normal size.

"The car!"

Xander bit his lower lip and it looked like he was tearing up. "Totaled."

"But you're both alive, and that's what matters," Mona rushed to add.

Jackson rubbed his eyes and looked for the bed controller to move into a sitting position. "Compton?"

"That man is behind bars where he should have been a long time ago," Dave Carter said as he walked into the room holding a carrier full of styrofoam cups. He distributed the drinks to Mona and Xander. He bent down to hug Jackson.

"Ow!"

"Sorry. Good to see you awake, Jax." He exchanged a look with Mona. "Really good. I can go back down to the cafeteria if you want something."

Jackson shook his head. "What happened?"

"Do you remember going to Compton's office?" Xander asked.

Jackson nodded.

"And the plane ticket?"

Jackson frowned, then smiled. "Mom got the PayPal email?"

Xander pulled up a chair and sat down. "Yeah. When she called and I didn't pick up, she called Ben. He told her about our appointment with Compton. Then he saw my check in and called 911."

Mona took over. "I called, too, and drove to meet them." She gave Xander a look. "And needless to say, I've changed my

PayPal password. Josh had called 911 as soon as he saw your message, sweetie. The police did check out the Digital Capital building. You were gone, but the state of the office was enough to make them believe there was something going on."

"What about . . .," Jackson squinted, then closed his eyes for a moment. He couldn't quite retrieve what he wanted to say, like the image of it was there, but the words were gone. "The police email? Did that work, or was that a bluff?"

Xander grimaced. "Spam blocker. How do the police expect to get any electronic evidence if they automatically block all attachments?"

"But why?" He turned to Xander. "Were you right?"

"Aren't I always?" Xander grinned and Dave nudged him. "Well, maybe I didn't know everything."

"Xander was right about Compton manipulating StemPunk and SpitTake to humiliate his partners and blast their bottom line," Dave said as he sat down on the edge of the bed, "but there was more going on. His wife had accused him of hiding assets when they divorced a couple years ago, and the scandal made the news, but they settled out of court with a binding agreement on both sides not to reveal the terms."

Jackson realized he wasn't really following what his dad was saying. He wasn't sure if it was because it was all new, because he was so foggy, or because he was beginning to feel like someone had beaten him with a baseball bat.

"So?"

Dave's mouth twitched into a smile. "So he was in financial trouble and had been on the radar of the SEC, among others, for actions he was taking to remedy that situation."

"It was like . . . insider trading?" Jackson asked.

"Sort of," Xander said. He looked at their dad. "He was definitely manipulating stock value by sharing information. Some of it just wasn't true."

"Huh." Jackson wasn't entirely following. "Do you think I could get some Ibuprophen? Or Tylenol?" He coughed and winced. "Or morphine?"

"Are you in pain? Is it bad?" Mona sounded very distressed as she clasped his hand.

Jackson took a deep breath and produced a smile. "It's not that bad. But if I can have something . . ."

"I'll ring the nurse," Mona said.

Jackson looked from face to face; his family looked tired and relieved and happy. Maybe too happy.

"How long have I been . . . out?"

Mona and Dave exchanged a look. "It's been almost two days," Mona said.

"Two days?"

"Yeah, you've really been larding," Xander said.

"So it wasn't just the leg?"

Mona squeezed his hand. "You got stuck, and Xander pulled you out . . . but one foot was still in partial contact with the car when the train hit. You got a spiral fracture and the impact threw you almost to the fence. Because Xander was holding your arms, he got thrown, too."

"You totally kneed me in the balls," Xander said, caught his mother's look and said, "I mean groin. And I got a concussion. Maybe not as bad as yours, but still."

"I'm pretty sure you deserved it."

Jackson pointed to his cast. "They fixed it though, right? I mean, there isn't any . . . permanent damage?" He looked from his mother to his father and back again.

"You'll be fine," Mona smiled. "You'll be on crutches for a quite awhile, though."

"And no sports for the rest of the year," Dave added.

"There is some good news, though," Xander said. "Pigs for Peace made it to the final three in the pitch contest."

Jackson started to shake his head, then thought better of it. "Of course it did." He gave Xander the smirk guaranteed to get a rise out of him. "Good thing you listened to me."

"Fail!" Xander twitched, but didn't touch Jackson. "I did all the work, loner."

"Yeah," Jackson said. "You keep telling yourself that, bro.

Epilogue

"Seriously, I think I've got at least a couple more days of sympathy leniency on my homework."

Jackson was sitting at a picnic table with his friends eating lunch. Josh was using his crutches to race up and down the walkway trying to break his speed record.

"Dude!" Jackson yelled at him. "You are going to actually need those if you don't stop."

"Aw, Jax, I didn't know you cared," Josh said, plopping down on the bench and picking up his sandwich.

Jackson gave an exaggerated shrug. "I don't. I just don't want to have to find someone else to carry my stuff." He laughed and leaned sideways as Josh reached over to punch him in the shoulder.

"Swing and a miss!" Ethan said.

"Trolled," Xander said in a bored voice as he walked up to the table. "I'm staying late for journalism," he said to Jackson. "Mom will pick you up after school."

"Congratulations on that pig . . . app . . . thing," Nicholas said.

Xander acknowledged the comment with quick chin lift. "Thanks, man."

Jackson wiped his mouth and crumpled his napkin. "I can hang out and watch practice."

"That's okay," Xander said, "I've got a ride home."

A smile spread slowly across Jackson's face until it became a grin. "With Emily, maybe?"

"Oooh . . ." Jackson's friends supplied a falsetto Greek chorus.

Xander flushed and turned to Ben, who had joined him. "Not having a car sucks." He looked back at Jackson. "Or maybe it's just having a brother that sucks."

Jackson looked past Xander and gestured with his chin. Xander, Ben, and all the freshmen turned.

"Xander? Jax? May a speak with you for a moment?" Dr. Warner had been avoiding the boys since the whole meth accusation, or at least that's how it seemed to them.

Jackson reached for his crutches, but his friends stood and started clearing their paper plates and lunch bags. "We're done anyway," Josh said.

"Um, yeah," Ben said, "I've got . . . a . . . thing . . ," he turned abruptly and hurried off in the direction of the computer lab.

Xander sat beside Jackson and Dr. Warner sat across from them. She looked to her right and left as if checking for eavesdroppers, then clasped her hands and leaned forward. Jackson raised his eyebrows at Xander.

"I'm sorry I . . . declined to help you when you asked," she began, "especially considering what happened." She met Jackson's eyes then quickly looked away. "I know I have no right to ask you for anything. . . ." Her voice trailed off.

Xander started drumming his fingers on his leg. Jackson watched Dr. Warner's face. She spoke toward her own hands at first, then looked directly at Xander.

"But it isn't for me." Dr. Warner stood, made a subtle gesture with her hand, then extended it. "Please don't hold the referral against her. And thank you for . . ." she let the sentence hang, and Xander took her hand and shook. She turned to shake Jackson's hand, then walked away.

A tall thin blonde with eyes so pale they were nearly colorless slid into the space Dr. Warner had vacated. It was Carrie Davis, a senior.

"Hi, Xander," she said, "and you're . . ."

"Jax."

"Nice to meet you, Jax." Carrie smiled with the sort of autopilot politeness that all teenagers learned when they started interviewing for college if they hadn't picked it up before. Then her face became serious.

"Dr. Warner said you might be able to help me . . ."

"Do you need a website? Jailbreak?" Xander asked.

Jackson shielded his face with one hand so she couldn't see him rolling his eyes.

"I . . . no! What?" Carrie looked confused, then took a deep breath and continued. "This is going to sound weird, but . . . it's the guy my mom is seeing. There's something off about him." She hooked her long straight hair behind her ears. "There's nothing concrete. When you google him, he looks legit. Well, legit for what little there is." She paused and wrapped her arms around herself as if she were cold. "But he gives me the creeps. I don't think he is who he says he is."

Xander's fingers stopped drumming. Identity theft, encrypted data unraveling, and finessed hacking opportunities passed before his eyes like the multi-window display on Black Ops. He saw Jackson smiling out of the corner of his eye.

Xander nodded once. "We're in."

The End

Acknowledgements

The Carter Bros would not exist without my sons, Max and Alex, and their friends, whose relationships and conversations inspired and enlivened this story.

Thanks to John Billheimer, Mark Coggins, and Ann Hillesland for the monthly critique and support, and to the Unabridged Book Club: Jan Austin, Alexia Gilmore, Teri Hessel, Barrie Moore, and Jeanese Snyder for their laughter, love, and helpful feedback.

Additional sources of inspiration, motivation, and feedback include Susan Giovanni, Elliot Foad, Jennifer Allen, and Taylor Bruce.

Big smoochies to John Banning, who makes all things possible.

This is a work of fiction. That means I made it all up. There are infusions of real locations and incidents to provide a plausible framework for the story, but any resemblance to actual people is either imaginary or pure narcissism.

About the Author

Sheila Scobba Banning lives in the San Francisco Bay Area with her husband, sons, and a menagerie of pets. When not writing, Sheila creates fascinators and outlandish hats, throws fabulous parties, spends way too much time volunteering at school, and laughs until she cries every day. Her superpower is catalysis.